The .

The Post Road

Tierney Steele

The Post Road
Tierney Steele

ISBN 979-8-9858581-8-1

Cover design by Liz Delton

This is a work of fiction. The characters and events in it are inventions of the author. Any resemblance to actual persons or events is entirely coincidental.

For Chris, without whom this book could not have been written

Special thanks to Liz Delton

1. Normal Like You

Mully idled in her best friend's driveway and marveled at how pretty "golden hour" could make even a boring suburban street look. House after house was set up on a hill with brick or concrete steps leading down to the driveway and garage, the only variation being what type of small tree each homeowner had planted next to their stairs. Mully glanced back up at the still-closed front door and suppressed a sigh before deciding to turn on the radio. Static filled the car. Thanks to the hills that made up her hometown, the station that came in perfectly at her house was completely blocked here. She stabbed the seek button a few times. Talking, rap, talking, classic rock, more static... As the numbers spun back around to the start of the FM band she admitted defeat.

Flipping down her sun visor, Mully didn't even have to look to pull the CD she wanted from the holder strapped there. With her other hand, she opened the compartment between her seat and the passenger side and got out her Discman. After loading the CD in, she pulled out the magic that made it all work: a cassette aux cord that went into the tape player of her car. She hit play on the car dashboard, pressed play on the Discman, and sat back to relax and wait as the opening chords of Everclear's "So Much for the Afterglow" filled the vehicle.

She picked at the frayed edge of her denim shorts, her eyes wandering down her legs to her Doc Martens. Mully worked at her father's gas station and repair shop, and his strongest rule was no open-toe shoes *ever,* under any circumstances. For two summers now, she had the tan line around her calves to prove that she obeyed. The black boots matched the chipped black nail polish on her fingers and the black dyed hair growing out in her ponytail. Despite all the black, she would never consider herself a Goth—nor would anyone else. Mully was also wearing her favorite green Star Wars t-shirt; she had been an optimistic, Jedi-loving, believer in friendly aliens since she first got into the movies as a kid. No, Mully wasn't really anything as far as high school stereotypes went. Technically a drama kid... but she was a techie, so that didn't really fit. She was good with computers... but had no interest in coding or anything like that. She didn't party, she didn't play sports... Really, all Mully cared about was making movies.

There was finally a bang as the front door of the house shut. Mully smiled up at the one other person who got it. AJ had just been another boy in her class, someone she was aware of but never really got to know, until they started middle school and were assigned their lockers. Since his last name was Cadwallyn and her last name was Carr, they had spent seven years next to each other. She was the one who started calling him AJ instead of Adam. It stuck. Then they discovered the *X-Files,* taping every episode off the TV so they could watch over and over again. They had even dressed up as Mulder and Scully for Halloween freshman year—complete with red hair for Mully, the first of many times she would dye it a different color from its natural blonde. AJ had looked at his short female friend with her red hair and thought about calling her Scully, but she was just such a Mulder that he slurred it into Mully. That had stuck too. So Adam and Josephine had become AJ and Mully... and never looked back.

That felt like a lifetime ago, even though it had only been four years, and now, here was AJ headed towards her car trying not to drop his CD binder and a couple of flannel shirts while simultaneously shoving his keys into his pocket.

He was tall and skinny and drowning in slightly baggy jeans and a shapeless collared mechanic's shirt. It was one of hers, as the name-patch "Joey" proved. He wore Chucks and had a Captain Crunch whistle on his keychain... and he didn't really fit in anywhere either. His hair was short and neat. He hardly ever swore and had no interest in drinking. He could rattle off the specs of any spaceship in the Star Wars movies, but that had never seemed like a useful skill until he got to know Mully. She had encouraged him to write his own sci-fi stories, and before long, they were making movies together. And pretty well, too. Earlier this year, AJ's work won a regional competition. It had been a nice boost right before graduation. Then there was the long boring summer to get through before tonight–the last night before leaving for college.

He opened the back door to toss his CDs and shirts on the backseat, and Mully leaned over to greet him.

"Hi kid, you famous yet?" she asked as usual.

AJ ignored her as he let himself into the passenger side, but did mutter, "Sorry 'bout the wait," as he buckled his seatbelt.

"Having dinner?"

"No, dinner would have required all members of my family to be in the same room at the same time." He was spitting out the words, and she knew she should back off and let him decompress before saying anything else.

But she couldn't stop herself from following up. "Your

dad and Jack?"

"Jack doesn't come out of his room during daylight," AJ snorted. He waited for Mully to put her car in reverse and look out the back before he went on, "My mom and dad are so stupid. They were at it again. Like, how will their fighting convince Jack to get a job? What do they think will even happen?"

"You're supportive."

"Like a jock strap," he snapped.

Mully stared at him for a moment, and then decided it wasn't worth pointing out that he was being an asshole to her. His family was kind of a mess these days and she tried to stay out of it. She started accelerating down his street and changed the subject.

"What are those, really?" she asked. "I mean, I get the general idea, but how—"

"I'm not discussing this with you."

"Fine," Mully shrugged, "Leave me in ignorance." She and AJ had an unspoken but no less real rule that they didn't discuss sex or biology or what physically made them different from each other. But every now and then it was fun to test him, to see if he would slip up and admit something gross.

"You'll survive," was all he said in response.

"I got a good purring for you today."

In response to AJ's confused look, Mully half-shrugged toward the backseat while still deftly steering along the winding back roads. AJ turned and spotted the mini-recorder lying there. Beaming, he retrieved it and pressed play. A short clip of an engine repeatedly revving and dying competed with Everclear to fill the car. A thoughtful smile played across AJ's face; he was probably already thinking about how he could best use the audio.

After a respectful silence, Mully explained, "This big ass pickup came into the station and let me record it."

"This is awesome. You're a regular Ben Burtt."

"Some good had to come of me pumping gas all summer." She used her blinker as she turned onto yet another tree-lined suburban street with cars parked all along the curbs. "I'm just sorry I won't be here to help make the final product."

"Return to M'lik: The First Tale of the Suffolkenisis without Mully," AJ laughed. "What a catchy title."

"You know, for someone who doesn't believe in aliens, you sure write a lot of science fiction," she couldn't resist pointing out.

"It's a metaphor," AJ said.

"Or maybe you're finally starting to beli—"

He cut her off. "I will never get over you being smarter than me. Seriously. I think the SATs were rigged. And—hey, watch out!"

AJ himself was cut off as they made an unprotected left onto the main drag and Mully had to yank the wheel to keep them in the left-most lane as a car they both recognized pulled up alongside them.

AJ rolled down his window and yelled, "Trin, you maniac!"

Katrina Edlund, a fellow recent Norford High graduate, was batting away the fuzzy dice that hung from her rearview mirror which had attacked her when she had to pull into the right lane. Her bright blue Volvo 850 matched her hair, and when she rolled down her window to yell back at them, Reel Big Fish blared out into the summer evening.

"Nice left Mully!" Trin shouted.

"If you hadn't been speeding, my calculations would have been correct!" Mully fired back.

With a grin, Trin darted her eyes between them and the road as she said, "What, were you going 88 miles per hour?"

As they came to a red light, both girls slowed to a stop.

"The usual?" Trin asked.

"Yeah, see you there," AJ answered.

The light turned green and Mully hesitated a moment so that Trin could pull ahead into her lane. AJ rolled his window back up, acting like turning the handle was the hardest thing in the world.

"You're a total weakling," Mully pointed out.

"Your car is too old to exist," he countered.

Mully affectionately patted the dash. She adored her car, despite—or maybe because of—the fact that it was almost as old as she was. Her white car may have predated power windows or locks or even cup holders coming standard, but to Mully, that was a small price to pay to drive an actual Jaguar. "You're a good car," she crooned. "Don't listen to the carless jealous fool."

"Who's more foolish, the fool or—"

"Seriously AJ?"

"You can't tee that up and expect me to ignore it," he complained.

They actually managed three seconds of peacefully cruising down the Post Road, but then Mully couldn't stop herself from saying, "Poor Trin."

"Huh?"

"Stuck staying here to go to Willer," she clarified.

AJ was quick to answer. "Oh, you mean one of the best schools in the country *and* her dad works there, so she's practically going for free?"

"But we all swore we'd get out of here," Mully burst

out.

"We made that pact when we were fifteen," AJ said quietly, a hint of warning in his words.

They had been sitting in sophomore English class, rolling their eyes at some jock making fart jokes about *Inherit the Wind*, and the three of them all swore they would get out of Norford as soon as they could. Go to college out of state. Never look back.

Now, AJ's voice was just the littlest bit raised as he turned towards Mully and said, "Just because you decided to go to school on the other side of the country doesn't mean Trin is *stuck* here. We were kids, and we didn't know anything about how expensive college is. It was a stupid thing to say, anyway."

"I didn't see you applying to any in-state schools."

"I didn't see you even considering New York with me before you decided on USC."

"I didn't see *YOU* considering USC!" Mully yelled, then reined herself in. This was a stupid argument and she was sick of having it. AJ ignored her and looked out the window.

Mully didn't say anything else. She couldn't understand why every time they had hung out together this summer, they ended up sniping at each other. AJ was her best friend in the world, and she knew he looked forward to getting out of the house and away from his family all day. So why couldn't they go more than twenty minutes without arguing? Especially today: tonight was their last night together before they split up to go to college. Mully sighed. AJ slumped deeper into his seat and kept his eyes focused on the stores flashing by as Mully headed west on the main road through town.

2. Freedom Like a Shopping Cart

As they sped down the Post Road that ran through the middle of town, Mully and AJ flipped down their sun visors when the angle of the setting sun got in their eyes.

Two lanes in each direction, the road expanded at most stoplights with turn-only lanes that made it nearly as wide as the highway. Shopping plazas full of stores and restaurants lined both sides of the road. It was the geographical center of town, and also the center of all the action. On either side, suburban neighborhoods spread out, punctuated by schools and baseball diamonds for Little League teams. There was a middle school north of the Post Road and a middle school south of it. A slightly industrialized area had grown up one block over from the train station, with warehouses and a factory or two. The best pizza place in town had picnic tables with plastic red checkered tablecloths outside and a view over the Norford River. There were well-planned residential neighborhoods, with straight streets named after trees or flowers or founding fathers, and there were neighborhoods of twisty back roads only wide enough for one car at a time, with mangled Native American words for names. Dead-ends and cul-de-sacs were popular in both types of neighborhoods.

This being Connecticut, the Post Road was the only space wide-open enough to really see more than one block at a time. Most of the town was covered in trees: woods that ran up into people's backyards, maple trees dropping enough leaves in the fall to keep teenagers busy raking for weeks, and the ever-present deer fences... and the deer that ignored them.

But the deer were too smart to go near the Post Road and its busy traffic. They stuck to the neighborhoods and yielded the main road through town to its human residents. In the mornings, the road was full of station wagons and minivans of people running errands. By afternoon, the cars on the road were more eclectic. By night? By the time the glowing sun stopped shining down the strip of asphalt blinding half the drivers, the road was given over to the young people. The teenagers with nothing better to do. Too old to have to be home when the streetlights came on, but too young to have anywhere to go. And so they drove. Up and down the Post Road. Sometimes with a destination in mind; sometimes just to be out of their houses.

It had been a long summer full of such evenings, and Mully saw no reason tonight would be any different. She knew exactly how long each light was and the braking distance between every block, but Mully didn't really know much about the road itself. Sure, back in elementary school she had been taught the history of it, but the only two facts that stuck were that the Post Road ran from New York City to Boston and that it was designed for mailmen. Or something like that. It was all mixed up in her brain with the burning of 1812 and Mohicans and George Washington and their fourth-grade teacher making actual venison stew for them to try after reading *Sarah, Plain and Tall.*

The next year, Mully had discovered movies, specifically that there were people who *made* them, and everything she had learned before that was just a vague memory. Except the venison stew, which she had found utterly disgusting. After that, she declared herself a vegetarian and never looked back.

Mully drove past the grocery store and thought about how she could remember the exact shade of gray the sky had been while her mom sat waiting for the light to make the left-hand turn into the parking lot. She was anxious to get the shopping done before it started raining in earnest, and Mully had been trying to explain that she wasn't going to eat animals anymore. She hadn't even known the word for it at that point. Mully's mom finally made the turn and said, "So you're a vegetarian now?" as she found a parking space. Although Mully was pretty sure she had rolled her eyes and cursed under her breath, that was the end of it. Her parents might think it was weird, but they had never tried to stop her. The same way they didn't really understand *why* she wanted to make movies, but as long as her grades stayed decent, they were happy to keep her supplied in DV-8 tapes. And of course, they had been so proud when she got into USC film school, even though it meant that tomorrow the baby of the family would move to the other side of the country.

It would be fine. It had to be: she would be on a plane in less than twenty-four hours. Mully tamped down the slightly-panicked feeling welling up inside her as she drove past more stores. She didn't even have to look out the window to know exactly what they were passing on their way to meet Trin. First the liquor store. The "head shop", as her dad still called it. The diner that made the best chocolate chip pancakes in the world, and right across the street, the diner that made AJ's favorite hamburger. Then past the banquet hall, where all their formal high school dances had been held. The photographer's shop was so close to that building that they even shared a parking lot. Then came the toy store, the bookstore, the place to buy sports equipment, and the place to buy CDs. Mully sped past what used to be the Caldor her mom was working at when she met Mully's dad, and the next plaza that once contained the drugstore and fabric shop that her mom's parents worked at when *they* met back in the '50s. Now she just thought of them as the shoe store and the party supply store. Past that was the army-navy store. The Chinese food. The pizza place. A few fast food options. The fancy-but-not-too-fancy restaurant you got taken to for celebrating a particularly good report card. She knew every inch of the road because she had never lived anywhere else.

Ignoring the ramp onto I-95, Mully continued down the Post Road and finally turned into the parking lot of her destination. Pulling into a spot directly under the giant red sign, she felt another pang of nostalgia as she got out of the car. She must have made thousands of trips here with her grandparents, always finishing up with a clown sundae, no matter the time of day. She had felt so fancy with her long-handled ice cream spoon clinking against the silver dish. For a moment, Mully was frozen half in-half out of her car as she realized that at some point she had stopped coming here with her grandparents and started coming here with her friends instead.

"You ok?" AJ asked across the car roof.

"Yeah, fine," she said tersely, shaking the wave of sadness off. Mully pushed down her lock and closed the car door.

3. La Vie Boheme

Mully and AJ were used to popping down the locks in their doors as they climbed out. Mully lovingly ran a hand along the trunk of her white 1986 Jaguar XJ6, in pristine running condition, with only a "Follow the White Rabbit" bumper sticker to show it belonged to a teen. It was the only classic Jaguar in the county and possibly the only one from the '80s in the state. Her mother had kept it in great shape through the years, but any car over a decade old was considered ancient. Mully didn't care. It was the first car she had ever taken care of herself and she was sure that this was the best vehicle ever produced by man, even if it did require her to keep a special set of tools around just to avoid stripping its screws whenever anything needed fixing.

Trin had already gotten out of her bright-blue car and came bouncing across the parking lot toward them. It would be impossible to guess just by looking at her that she was also college-bound. Shorter even than Mully, with a round face and dimples, it didn't matter that Trin was actually a few months older than her friends. She would always look like a kid next to them. Katrina Edlund wore red Converse high-tops covered in writing (both Sharpie and pen) that were almost completely hidden by her baggy jeans. She had to hitch these back up as she walked. Trin wore a wide, studded belt, but it couldn't work miracles; she basically had no hips for her jeans to hang onto. The waistband of said jeans didn't quite meet the bottom of her blue Blink-182 butterfly t-shirt. Trin tossed her keys, wallet, and bulky flip phone into the button-covered messenger bag she brought everywhere. This she slung across her body as they walked across the parking lot.

"Last night, right?" she said to Mully.

"I'm out of here at 11:45 tomorrow morning."

"I can't believe it's really happening," Trin said, shaking her head, still in disbelief that her best friend of four years was about to move to Hollywood.

"You'll be..." Mully trailed off. "Fine," she finished a beat too late. She had no idea what to say and she didn't want to be a bitch and blurt out something rude about Trin being stuck here to her face.

Trin linked arms with Mully as they passed through the outer door that AJ held open for them. "It's only an hour on the train to the city, so I'm going to be down there bugging Ana and AJ all the time. Right AJ?"

His answer was drowned out as Mully pulled open the inner door and the noise of a crush of people in the entrance area blasted them. The restaurant was packed with families finishing dinner and high school kids fueling up for a night out. A group of middle-school-ish aged kids were gathered around the claw machine, shouting instructions to the boy who had sacrificed two quarters for a try. He bit his lip in concentration as he pushed the buttons.

Mully didn't bother to watch his defeat. She caught the hostess's eye and put her hands together in prayer. The college-aged girl rolled her eyes, but only a couple minutes later, led them over to their usual window booth in the front corner of the restaurant. Yes, it was crowded next to the pile of highchairs and booster seats, but it allowed them to see the whole of the restaurant *and* watch the parking lot.

"Who has money?" Mully asked before her butt even touched the seat.

"Aren't you paying since it's your last night and you worked all summer?" AJ asked with a grin.

Mully didn't return it. "Yeah right! You know my dad only agreed to hire me if I saved it for college. And it's not like I earned a lot to begin with. Making change, pumping gas for confused moms from Jersey... yeah, that's the ticket to riches." She pulled her wallet out of her left back pocket and held it open as proof.

As she stuffed it back into her pocket, she yelped, then pulled out a small ring of keys. "Oh, right!" She handed them to a bewildered Trin. "Here you go."

"What's this?"

"They never took my keys back after Drama. That's the auditorium, the prop room, and the side door on the music hallway. Use them well."

Trin looked unsure. "Use them... Shouldn't we give them back to the school?"

"They never asked for them," Mully shrugged. "Finders keepers." She had been Stage Manager for so long that she no longer thought of the keys as "belonging" to the school anyway. The auditorium was more like an extension of her house than a part of her school.

Trin nervously chewed on her lip as she threaded them onto her keychain and shoved everything back into a pocket of her messenger bag. She had spent just as many hours doing Drama as anyone else, but she had never been in charge. Even though she had run the lights, sewn costumes, and even appeared on stage, Trin had never had the same feeling of ownership that Mully did as Stage Manager.

Mully had turned back to AJ to ask him if he was really

going to make yet another sequel to his prize-winning sci-fi story, but she didn't get a chance.

"Hey, Ana made it," Trin announced, jerking her head at the window in the direction of a car pulling into the parking lot.

"How'd she know we'd be here?" Mully asked in surprise.

"Are you kidding me?" AJ scoffed. "We've had dinner here every Friday this summer. And last summer. And before that, our parents probably had dinner here every Friday of their summers. And before that, their parents!" Then he lapsed predictably into quoting one of his favorite classic movies, "*And you were there! And you were there! And you!*"

He pointed suddenly at the waitress, who practically dropped their three waters onto their table in surprise. She took off as fast as she could away from them. AJ ignored her alarm and popped a straw into one of the glasses so he could hydrate after his outburst.

"What I'm saying is, we're boring," he finished. He slid his finger over the top of the straw, then pulled it out of the cup. He carefully let out one drop of water at a time onto his scrunched up straw wrapper. The water caused the wrinkles to open, making the wrapper look like a worm come to life on the table. As if to prove his point about being boring, Trin and Mully ignored his trick and watched out the window as Ana parked her car.

It was a 1997 BMW 318i and Mully sighed as she wished for the thousandth time that Ana would wash her car more often. It wasn't *dirty*... it just needed a quick cleaning. Take all that garbage that built up on the floors and in the cup holders out and vacuum... It was the least she could do for such a wonderful car.

Ana Foster never thought of it that way. She was just happy to have her own car. She had been borrowing her parents' cars when she could, driving her little sisters places as an excuse to get behind a wheel, but that all seemed worth it when her eighteenth birthday present was a brand new BMW. What was the big deal if she popped an empty coffee cup underneath the passenger seat on the drive to school in the morning? Who cared if there were always at least three half-drunk water bottles rolling around on the floor? It was her car, after all.

Ana hopped out and locked up with the key fob. As she hurried across the parking lot, she smirked a little, her pace telling the world she knew she looked good. Mully could barely remember a time when Ana *didn't* turn the heads of everyone she passed. Tonight, eighteen, in a black tank top, denim shorts, and black chunky slides, she strode up to the restaurant door like she owned this town. Which she kind of did. See, lots of girls are plenty cute, but only a few are really pretty in the everyday real world. That meant that when someone was actually beautiful, like Ana Foster, they seemed stunning to the normal population. Every heterosexual boy in Norford High School considered himself lucky that he had simply gotten to be in Ana's presence for four years.

With that attention came, well, not-so-great attention. Mully knew Ana had built up quite the strong defenses since puberty and Ana knew how to take care of herself. It was this self-esteem that allowed her to hold her sunglasses in her mouth, pull her hair up into a ponytail, walk right past the hostess and over to their booth, then take the sunglasses out of her mouth so she could kiss her boyfriend—all while he was wearing some other girl's shirt.

Ana slid in next to AJ and directed "How's it going?"

to him. She shrugged off her black faux leather mini-backpack and dropped it onto the booth seat next to her.

"We just got here," he said by way of answer.

She turned to talk to Trin and Mully, but before she even opened her mouth, a waitress came up to the table.

Having scared off the person who was actually covering this section tonight, the foursome now had to deal with Ellen Carr, Mully's older sister. She had been working here off and on since she turned sixteen, and now that she was in college, she was even more motivated to make money during her summers. Ellen was twenty-two and took much better care of herself than Mully, but no one could actually look good in the white button-down shirt tucked into black polyester pants uniform that she had to wear at work.

Ellen's blonde hair was pulled back in a severe bun and she was careful not to dislodge any hair as she tucked her pen away over her right ear. She put both hands on her hips before saying in a steady, vaguely-threatening voice, "Are you guys going to actually order something tonight?"

"What could you be implying?" Mully asked, her voice full of fake innocence.

"I'm not kidding. I can't comp whole dinners tonight guys."

Ana didn't blink an eye. "Patty melt, waffle fries, and a coke."

"Can I share?" AJ asked.

"Two melts, two cokes," Ana amended.

"Just a chocolate Frib please," Trin said.

"You really won't spot me a grilled cheese?" Mully asked her sister in shock.

Ellen rolled her eyes and shook her head no.

"Boy," Mully shook her head, feigning sadness. "Your

own sister..."

Ellen looked down at her pain-in-the-ass baby sister and, without thinking, said the worst thing possible. "Please don't make a scene."

She realized her mistake immediately, but it was too late. Mully sat up straight, invigorated, and burst into song. "La Vie Boheme" from *Rent*, specifically.

"Oh no," Ellen whispered as Trin leaped in to join her. Within moments, all four of them were taking turns with the lines, ignoring the stares of the people around them, singing with glee about teas and Akitas.

"I hate all of you," Ellen said even though they weren't listening. She headed off to put their order in.

If Ellen thought depriving them of an audience would stop them, she was wrong. Like all true theater kids, once Mully, Trin, AJ, and Ana began singing, they had no intention of stopping.

Ana's trained voice put the others to shame, but they were having a grand old time as the families nearby became more and more uncomfortable. When Mully reached the line "Hey mister, she's my sister!" she stood and pointed across the restaurant to Ellen who continued to ignore them. Ellen was too busy bracing herself. She knew all the words too—

"MUCHO MASTURBATION!" yelled every teenager in the restaurant. Mully and her friends were giggling hysterically when Ellen put their plates down on the table a bit harder than was technically necessary. But she'd added an order of fries for her sister.

4. History of a Boring Town

After dinner, Ana was the one who went up to pay at the front counter. As her friends squeezed past on their way outside, Trin handed over a five-dollar bill to at least help. Mully looked a little guilty as she held the door for Trin.

"Hey, wait a sec," Ellen called as she rushed over to them. She thrust a paper bag into Mully's free hand and hissed, "You still all suck though."

"You're a peach," Mully said to Ellen's back as she retreated into the kitchen. She followed Trin outside, hugging the warm bag to her chest. Trin ignored AJ standing next to Mully's car; instead she popped open her trunk. Trin and Mully settled themselves on the edge to enjoy the grilled cheese sandwiches Ellen had given them.

"I need to get my CDs," AJ told Mully. She tossed him her keys without a word.

Ana had just reached the car to join them. "Speaking of CDs," she said, "I made you a going-away present." Ana pulled a jewel case from her bag and handed it to Mully. "Lots of Cali songs. I think."

"Thank you!" Mully said through a mouthful of food.

"I can't believe you're leaving tomorrow," Ana added.

Mully swallowed quickly and said, "You're leaving tomorrow too."

"Yeah, but I'm driving into the city, not flying to the other side of the country," Ana said, waving off the comparison.

"You're taking your car?" Mully asked through another bite.

"Oh, no, I can't have it at school even if there was somewhere to park. My parents are dropping me off. Will you drive yours out to California once you're a junior?"

Mully thought about it. "Not sure. Probably. It's going to be weird not having a car."

"A carless Carr?" AJ asked as he rejoined them with his CDs. He threw the keys back to Mully, which she caught one-handed without looking.

She ignored his question to razz him by holding up the CD Ana had given her. "Check it out AJ. It's the craziest thing: this mix has a list of what songs are on it! Can you believe it? Gee, I didn't think that sort of thing was even legal."

"Well, sure," he shrugged, "There's lots of room on a CD case."

"There is literally a lined piece of paper included with every blank tape you have ever bought. For that express purpose which you insist on ignoring." The giant pile of unlabeled cassette tapes in Mully's bedroom attested to AJ's refusal to write down what any one tape contained.

"If I list the tracks, it takes away from the mix, because then you'd be pre-judging it."

"I'm always pre-judging you."

No one bothered to point out to Mully that her retort didn't make any sense. AJ took the CD from Mully and looked it over. He smiled at Ana. "Good picks."

"Thanks."

They just stood there grinning at each other and might have stayed like that until the next Ice Age if Mully hadn't asked, "You guys taking off for a bit?"

They were the magic words, like Ana and AJ had just remembered that they were a couple and could go make out whenever they wanted.

"We'll meet up at the carnival, right?" Ana asked, already getting out her car keys.

"Sure," Trin and Mully said at the exact same time.

"See you!" Ana shouted over her shoulder as she hurried to her car with AJ.

The two girls watched in thoughtful silence as Ana and AJ drove off. Both were thinking "Must be nice" but didn't want to say it out loud in case it hurt the other girl's feelings. Instead, they finished up their sandwiches (Mully wiping her hands on her shorts, Trin using the paper bag as a napkin) and gathered up their garbage. Mully ran it over to the garbage can while Trin closed up her trunk.

"Do you want me to drive you over?" Trin offered.

"Nah, I want to drive while I can. I hadn't thought about how weird it will be to not have my own car at school." Mully shook her head to stop herself from wallowing in the thought. "Besides, no one will be at the carnival this early, so we've got time to kill."

"Ok, but we'll all meet there?" Trin clarified.

Mully wrinkled her forehead. "Of course," she said as she unlocked her car door. She couldn't figure out why Trin was being so insistent; the four of them had hung out practically every Friday night for the past four years, meeting up at a carnival or the movie theater and then spending the rest of the night together.

After starting their cars, both Mully and Trin rolled down their windows, allowing the music blasting from their stereos to battle. The horrendous mix of ska and metal blissfully only lasted a moment before each started driving. Mully pulled out onto the Post Road behind Trin, so she flashed her brights just for the hell of it. Trin gave her the middle finger in her rearview mirror. With a laugh, Mully pulled up next to her at the next red light.

"Guess you're turning right," Trin yelled over, gesturing at the street signs marking Mully's lane as "Right Turn Only".

"Guess so. Stay out of trouble!"

"See you later!" Trin said again.

Mully ignored the "No Turn on Red" sign and took off into a neighborhood of back roads. She carefully switched out her CDs one-handed to listen to the one Ana had given her, hoping for a song that would match her mood as she flew along the twisty roads.

Because flying is what it was. Brake before the curve, switch to gas at the apex. Almost lifting out of her seat as she went over a little hill in the road. The s-curves seemed to go on forever. Mully had never felt more at one with the world than behind the steering wheel of a car she trusted on these roads. She was so happy that she didn't even notice Ana's car parked with both occupants in the backseat as she blew past their old elementary school.

5. Dammit

Trin tried to enjoy listening to "Sugar Water" but she just couldn't get into it tonight. Not that she didn't like the song, but it wasn't a great one for driving around to. She continued along the Post Road, occasionally recognizing other students' cars. She would wave: sometimes they waved back, sometimes they ignored her. Eventually Trin realized she needed a change. She struggled to swap CDs without losing control of her car, but it was worth it to have something peppier playing when she made her U-turn to go back into town for another pass to look for someone to hang out with until it was time to meet her friends at the carnival.

She knew it was silly to feel so nervous about splitting up for an hour or so. Obviously the four of them would hang out tonight. It was what they did basically every Friday. But no matter how many years had passed since she became friends with Mully, there was always a little part of her that worried one day she'd go to meet her friends and... just... no one would show up.

Trin kept driving around, and on yet another pass down the Post Road, a dark car pulled up alongside her. Although Trin didn't recognize the vehicle, she knew the people inside. Joe Chu and Jerry Mazzerelli had been best friends since the second grade. Trin really got to know them starting in high school when they had both done drama. Jerry acted and Joe was a techie who had dated Mully for a few months junior year. Trin smiled as she looked over and saw that they were wearing their "Party on Wayne" and "Party on Garth" t-shirts. It was kind of reassuring to know that no matter how much was changing tomorrow, these guys were still best friend dorks that dressed in matching shirts.

She waved at them, and Jerry, who was driving, leaned his head out the window.

"How's it going?"

Trin shrugged. "Kind of boring tonight. But I'm meeting Mully and those guys at the carnival in a bit."

"What time is it?" Jerry shouted over. Trin shot him a puzzled glance. "The clock in here's been broken all summer, but my dad says it costs too much to bother fixing. I forgot my watch," he explained.

"Just turned 8. I'm going to start heading for the carnival. Want to come?"

Out of the corner of her eye, Trin saw Jerry and Joe exchange a look before Jerry stuck his head back out of the window.

"We just picked up a pizza so we're headed back to my house. But have fun!"

Jerry rolled his window back up to preserve his air conditioning. The guys waved before turning off the Post Road and Trin waved back. She sighed and drove along, wishing she had a best friend who just wanted to grab dinner then go home and watch movies or play video games all night.

As she passed the restaurant again, its parking lot still busy, Trin noticed Ellen getting out of work. The ugly uniform shirt was untucked and unbuttoned to show a white t-shirt underneath as she lit a cigarette and walked to her car. Although Trin had never really understood the love Ellen and Mully had for their cars, she did know that Ellen's red 1972

Porsche 911 was one of the coolest cars in the tri-state area. Most people assumed the Carr girls were spoiled, but Trin knew it had taken Ellen hours of unpaid labor at their dad's garage to restore it.

Trin was already several blocks ahead, but Ellen's car was so distinctive, so *red*, that she could see in her rearview mirror when Ellen turned left out of the restaurant parking lot, darting across six lanes of traffic to turn onto the Post Road. At the next light, Ellen banged another left to head home.

Trin wondered if she would go to the carnival too. Back before they could drive, Mully and Trin had often tagged along after Ellen when she went out on the weekend. A little part of Trin actually missed trying to sneakily watch Ellen and her boyfriend and whispering about what it must be like to be in high school. Now she knew... and soon she would know what it was like to be in college too.

6. Steal My Sunshine

There was a carnival almost every weekend during the summer. It started right after Memorial Day, usually in the big field next to Brookvalley Elementary School, and continued straight through until the weekend after Labor Day when the big slide and scrambler made their last appearances by destroying the soccer fields down by the water. That one had always been Ana's favorite because she liked going on the rides: the bigger and scarier, the better. Trin had always preferred the one at St. Ann's because cute firefighters set up a big tent selling food as an annual fundraiser. But Mully had never had a favorite. As long as she saw the usual rides and people, heard the usual music, and tasted the usual free samples of Sobe, Mully would have a fun night.

Tonight, Ana and Trin had settled for this weekend's entertainment: a small but busy carnival set up in the side parking lot of Norford High School. The Sobe cart was in its usual spot right by the ticket booth, and Mully and Trin had rushed straight over. Mully had just finished trying a new flavor when she spotted Ana and AJ making their way through the crowd towards them.

"It's the same set-up everywhere. Did you ever notice?" she heard AJ ask, and Mully flinched, knowing how annoyed Ana would be.

"It is NOT the same," Ana insisted, but instead of arguing her point, she just turned toward her other friends and ignored him.

Mully had been sneaking glances across the way at another group of kids. They'd all been in the same grade, so they'd known each other most of their lives. "I'll never get used to Johnny Morrill looking that good," she finally muttered.

"I wish he was going to Willer," Trin said, staring down into her cup instead of looking over at the hunk who also happened to be a star athlete and on his way to Yale after taking, like, seven AP classes last year. He had been a total geek and pretty good friends with AJ up through middle school, but around the same time AJ stopped going by Adam, John had discovered he was good at football and lacrosse, and they hadn't had anything to say to each other since.

"The rest of that group is going to Willer though," Ana said. "Derek, Will, Megan, Sarah—"

"Well at least you'll have plenty of pretty people to look at," Mully couldn't help cutting in. She hated thinking Johnny Morrill was cute. He was a walking Abercrombie & Fitch ad, and she knew she should hate him but... he just... smelled really good and she couldn't help it.

"Oh shut up," Trin said, her cheeks already bright red.

Mully caught AJ scowling and was about to change the subject when he blurted out, "So where are we going?"

"Uh, we're here?" Mully shrugged. It was a freaking carnival, after all.

"Let's go on the slide," AJ said, and the entire group did a double take. AJ usually had to be dragged onto rides.

"Fine by me," Ana said before he could change his mind, and quickly disappeared to go buy a handful of ride tickets.

That left Mully and Trin staring at AJ, who was

staring at the ground. Luckily, before it could get too weird, Trin shouted, "Hi Ellen!" and waved at Mully's older sister headed in their direction.

Ellen had changed into a ripped pair of jeans, a plain white tank top, and her old checkered slip-on Vans, yet she still managed to look nicer than the kids around her who had spent hours getting ready to see everyone. Instead of a bun, her hair fell softly to her shoulders, making her seem much less scary than she always was at work. Mully knew instinctively that her sister was pretty, but it still felt strange to see guys staring at her. Mully's face pulled into a frown, even though she was glad to see Ellen, because she wished Trin hadn't drawn so much attention to them.

Ellen walked over but was still looking around. "There's nobody here," she said over their heads.

"What am I, just a blur?" Mully said.

"I mean my age." Ellen continued scanning the crowd. Mully couldn't believe her sister hadn't recognized the lyric. Or maybe she did and was just so used to them quoting *Rent* that it didn't even register anymore. Ellen popped up onto her tip-toes to see further along the crowded walkway.

"Well Jack said he'd come out at some point," AJ said quietly.

"Oh great." Ellen thudded back down onto her heels. Without bothering to explain herself, she turned and walked over to buy a bottle of Sobe. Mully tried not to murder AJ. He *knew* Ellen wouldn't want to see his brother and now she'd probably ditch them the first chance she got.

But instead, Ellen rejoined the little gang, turning her bottle upside down and banging it with the butt of her palm. This left Mully free to go back to looking at Johnny Morrill but without trying to seem like she was looking. She shifted her weight from leg to leg, keeping moving so no one could follow her eye line. But of course she had underestimated her older sister once again.

"Hey, is that Johnny? Geez, he grew up. I thought he was your year." Ellen unscrewed the cap of her bottle and poured the sweet pina colada-like drink down her throat.

"He is." Mully tried to sound annoyed to be talking about him.

"Oh well," Ellen said with a smirk. Mully whipped her head up, about to tell her to back off. "Too young for me," Ellen added quickly.

"And that's Sarah and Megan with him," Trin said. "They've been in our classes off and on since kindergarten."

"But they suck," Mully added. Megan and Sarah were walking Abercrombie & Fitch ads too, but they were not as smart as Johnny and, if she was being honest, they had no redeeming qualities as far as she was concerned.

Trin opened her mouth to say something, but AJ spoke over her. "There's Blake Monroe. He's your age," he told Ellen.

"Oh, I don't know if I could..." Ellen blushed, something Mully had seen maybe twice in her whole life. Ellen took another swig of her drink, then rushed on. "I mean, we don't really know each other. Although he's... No. Um, I think I'm going to go over by the food and see who I can find." Ellen was still muttering her excuses as she walked away. Mully watched, amused as all hell, as her sister headed off. So the great and mighty Ellen Carr got embarrassed around hot guys too. It didn't matter if they weren't in high school anymore: the most popular boy of a class would always be intimidating to anyone who'd been at school with him.

Ana silently returned to their group, beaming, with

ride tickets in hand.

"Food sounds good," AJ said. Ana sighed and shoved the ride tickets in her mini-backpack as the two of them headed off in the same direction as Ellen.

"Catch you later," Ana tossed over her shoulder.

And with that, it was just Mully and Trin again. It wasn't that Mully didn't *like* hanging out with Trin, but she had been expecting to spend the evening with the whole gang. She sighed and ground her boot heel into the grass.

"Trin, what the hell was that?" she blurted. It came out meaner than she intended, but after hearing it out loud, Mully realized how angry she really was.

"What?" Trin asked, her face scrunched in confusion.

"*Hi Ellen,*" Mully mocked, waving and jumping up and down a couple times. "Stop sucking up to my sister. It's embarrassing."

Trin flushed red again but stood her ground. "Your sister is nice," she insisted.

"You just want to know someone at Willer next week," Mully spat out.

"Yes, Mully, I'm a total weirdo for wanting to know someone going to the same college as me. Obviously the NORMAL thing to do is move cross-country where I know nobody for hundreds of miles. That's healthy." Trin crossed her arms, but it twisted her messenger bag across her stomach and she settled for putting her hands on her hips instead.

"Oh come on." Heat rose in Mully's chest and she bit her lip, frustrated. She had been annoyed at Trin acting like her sister was the end-all-be-all, but she hadn't meant to make it a whole fight. Maybe she shouldn't have jumped up and down...

"No, it's not fair." Trin wasn't letting it go. "You're

completely changing your life and that's fine, but you don't get to act like it doesn't suck for the rest of us. I don't get why you just don't go to NYU with AJ and Ana. Lots of movies get made in New York City."

The heat building inside her reached Mully's face, and she felt like she was either going to cry or yell—so she started yelling at Trin. The words tumbled out of her as if someone else were saying them. "Seriously? I leave tomorrow and you're standing there telling me I should be going to a different college? Just so you could visit me? It's not happening. New York is awesome and I'm excited for AJ and Ana, but I am getting out of here." She had to stop and catch her breath.

"Well I'm not, and I choose to make other friends," Trin shot back as soon as Mully stopped speaking.

"Well go ahead," Mully challenged her.

"I will!"

"Fine!"

Mully turned around and focused all her attention on the first thing she saw, which happened to be the Frog Flip booth. She fished a crumpled dollar out of her pocket and slapped it on the counter before grabbing a hammer. *Perfect,* she thought, gripping it with two hands so she could really whack something and hopefully feel better.

7. Cannonball

Trin stood, in shock, as Mully completely ignored her. Then she hastily wiped her eyes before they could form actual tears. She had only seen Mully like this a couple times, and it was usually directed at AJ. Hopefully she'd be over it and stop acting like a jerk soon. In the meantime, though... Trin looked over the busy, loud carnival and wondered what to do with herself. Aqua's "Barbie Girl" was playing, and she wished Ana was still around. They loved to hate this song and knew all the lyrics. It was super fun to annoy AJ by singing it at him...

Trin shook her head. Ana and AJ had disappeared, probably making out somewhere. Mully was busy taking out her burst of anger on unsuspecting plastic frogs, and Trin would feel even more stupid if Mully knew she was still standing there. Thankfully, she thought of the group of people across the way. Ana had said a bunch of them were going to Willer. She gathered up all her gumption and walked over.

Johnny, Derek, and Will were having some sort of chugging competition in the middle of the circle of people with bottles of Sobe. Trin almost turned around but stopped when Johnny saw her approaching out of the corner of his eye and winked at her. Her brain started running wild. Why would he wink at her? Did he think she was cute? Did he think she was crazy? Had he ever said more than two words to her before? Did he even know who she was? Did he wink as a greeting?

Then she realized she was once again just standing there and made herself turn to the two nearest girls in the group cheering them on.

"Hi Megan. Hi Sarah."

Megan completely ignored her, but Sarah shifted slightly so Trin could join them. "Hey."

"I'm Trin."

"I... know?" Sarah looked confused. "Do you need something?"

"No. Umm, no. I just, I heard you're going to Willer and I'm going there too and I just wanted to say hi."

"Oh! Hi. Yeah, cool, right?"

"Yeah, cool." Trin wasn't sure what else to say.

"Are you going to live on campus?" Sarah asked, still keeping one eye on the boys. Derek ended up spraying a mist of his drink all over Johnny and Sarah wrinkled her nose in disgust.

"No, um, I'm going to live at home and save some money," Trin said despite Sarah's obvious lack of interest.

"Smart. But I'd lose my mind if I stayed at home. Do you know what you're going to study?"

"I'm not sure yet. I really liked acting but not enough to make a career of it, you know? Maybe English is the closest. But science is really cool too. I've always loved it, and after taking AP Chem it'd be weird to just stop." She could tell she was rambling but the words kept tumbling out. "But wouldn't it be cool to do something really random like archaeology? Or become a marine biologist? So I'll probably just get a bunch of gen eds out of the way to try everything for now." Trin had to gasp a little for breath. "You?" she asked Sarah.

Sarah was staring at her, mouth slightly open.

"History."

"Oh. Cool."

"Yeah. So, I gotta get going." The boys had finished and Megan was already herding them along.

"Yeah, of course, have fun."

"You too!" Sarah had to half-shout as she caught up with the group.

As soon as Sarah rejoined them, the group started laughing. They were all cracking up at something, and Trin tried not to notice the timing. She took a deep breath and told herself they were just laughing about the boys. Made sense. Besides, what would Sarah care if Trin talked too much? She always had, and no one had ever cared before. Talked too much, thought too much... Trin had always had a hard time making decisions and it showed in the way she interacted with the world. At least going to Willer had been an easy decision: her dad taught there, so it was way cheaper than any other school. And since she didn't know what she wanted to do with her life, a nice, normal college was all she needed. Right? Trin shook her head in frustration.

She turned to find Mully at the Frog-Flip booth, but she was gone. Trin went off to search for her. Mully could be kind of a jerk sometimes, but it was always short-lived and she didn't seem to mean it.

And Trin never had to worry that Mully was laughing at her.

8. Building a Mystery

Ellen walked slowly through the carnival, munching on fried clams. Somehow they always tasted better out of a red-and-white checkered paper basket than anything else. She looked around at the familiar lights, chuckled at the same old cheap prizes, and stopped right by the bottom of the big slide. She could see Mully thudding up the metal steps in those giant ugly boots of hers, AJ and Ana right behind her. Ellen saw Mully take a moment to look out over the carnival from the top of the slide and wondered once again what it must feel like to be brave enough to go all the way across the country to start life over at eighteen. She certainly had never made a decision like that.

Before Ellen could feel too depressed, AJ and Ana had caught up, and she watched the three of them spread out their burlap potato sacks at the top of each of the three lanes. Ellen grimaced as she imagined how scratchy the sacks felt against Mully and Ana's bare legs below their shorts.

She heard AJ in the middle lane shout, "Three, two, one, Geronimo!"

They launched themselves down the slide, racing and screaming with joy. Ellen shook her head, a little jealous at how much fun they were having.

"You are children," she teased as Mully danced in victory after reaching the bottom first. Mully stuck her tongue out, and the three of them rushed off to return their sacks to the pile next to the stairs. By the time they returned, they had picked up Trin too.

Ellen smiled. "Well kids, it's been fun," she said, as if she were their ancient elder instead of a college junior. She tossed her empty paper bowl into a nearby garbage barrel and tried to wipe her hands off on her jeans.

"Where are you going?" Mully asked quickly.

"The night is young, the moon is full, and I have better things to do than watch you throw up on the scrambler," Ellen answered.

"I won't throw up," Mully all but shouted at her.

"If you don't go on the scrambler," Ellen said as if finishing her sentence. "AJ, ladies, have a good night."

"You didn't say where you were going!" Mully yelled from behind as she walked away. "You know Mom will ask me!"

Ellen ignored her sister and wove through the crowds toward the front parking lot. She didn't even notice passing a group of young teenage boys, but some sixth sense made her look around, confused. She frowned as she became aware of a boy walking ever-so-slightly behind her. She watched him out of the corner of her eye. Some scrawny kid, shorter than her, swimming in his oversized t-shirt and long cargo shorts. Who the hell was this kid and why was he following her?

"Where you goin'?" the boy asked.

Ellen almost tripped over her own feet in surprise. "Huh?"

"You're leaving," he pointed out.

"Uh, yeah."

"Can I come with?" he asked. His eyes were wide with innocence, as if this was a perfectly normal thing to ask a complete stranger.

Ellen stared at him in utter confusion. He was even walking in step with her. In horror, she realized they had left the crush of the carnival behind and were now in an otherwise-empty and dark parking lot.

"Hey kid, where are your parents?" she asked him. Her gaze darted around as if two adults might magically appear. Her awareness of how far away everyone else was made her uneasy even though she wasn't sure why. This was probably the least threatening boy she'd ever talked to.

"I'm just here with some friends, but I'm ready to leave," he answered. Then he just stared at her, volunteering no further information.

"You can't... come with me..." Ellen struggled for words. "Who ARE you?"

"I'm Matt."

"Matt?"

"Laddie's brother," the kid clarified.

"Who's Ladd—" Ellen tried to ask.

"Anyway," he interrupted, "a whole bunch of us came together but this place is pretty lame," he continued.

"I don't think—"

"Couldn't you at least give me a ride home?"

"I—"

"Please?"

Ellen felt like her head was going to explode. She looked down at Matt's face and fought inside herself for the right thing to say.

"You're Matt?" she finally managed to get out.

"Yup." The streetlight on the edge of the parking lot made it look like he had a goddamn halo on top of his head.

"Laddie's brother?"

"And you're Mully's big sister, Ellen Carr, the coolest

girl in Norford."

She ignored his attempt to suck up to her.

"And you just want a ride home?" she said slowly, trying to convince herself this was an ok idea.

"I promise." Matt held up his right hand in the Boy Scout salute.

"Ok, ok, come on." She sighed but led him over to her car. Matt tugged on the passenger door handle, unaware that her car didn't have power locks. Ellen let herself in and leaned over to unlock his door.

"Your car is really small," Matt said as he sat down.

"It's a Porsche, kid. Don't you know anything?"

Matt's knees hit the bottom of the dash, knocking open the glove compartment. Ellen leaned over and slammed it shut, already regretting giving him a ride. He picked up the binder of CDs from the floor and started flipping through it.

"You sure have a lot of CDs."

"Yup." She pulled out a cigarette and put it between her lips.

Matt looked around, bewildered. "But there's no CD player in here."

"Jesus!" Ellen ripped the cigarette out of her mouth and gripped the steering wheel. She took a deep breath and explained, "That's because this car was built in the '70s, before they existed. We'll listen to the radio and we'll listen to the station I pick, got it?"

Matt was still flipping through the CD binder.

"Now look, look at me!" She got right up into his face and he stared back at her, a little terrified. "Ok, look into my eyes," she continued. "Do I look like someone who's kidding around?"

"No," Matt said meekly.

"Ok." She leaned back into her seat. "Ok. Put on your seat belt."

He did.

Ellen started the car and the radio came alive with Sarah McLachlan. Matt grimaced but said nothing. Ellen rolled down her window and lit her cigarette.

"Do you know anything about cars?" Ellen asked after a moment. She blew the smoke out the window and finally felt a little calmer.

"I know how to drive," Matt said just fast enough for her to be sure he was lying.

"What kind of car is this?" she asked.

"A... Porsche. Like you said." He gulped. The car was pulsing with silence, and when he couldn't take it anymore, he tried again. "A red Porsche?"

Ellen rested her head against the steering wheel for the briefest of moments, then straightened up. "This is a 911. A classic 911. We could be at sixty miles an hour in less than eight seconds." He was staring at her with a blank face. She knew it was snobby of her to think it, but she was completely shocked that someone wasn't impressed with her car. Usually you just had to say the word "Porsche" and guys started drooling. Instead, this kid just sat in her passenger seat, just... just blinking at her!

"That's very impressive," she said slowly.

"Sure, if you're into cars," he shrugged.

"Where do you live?" Ellen asked in defeat. She tapped her ash out the window.

"Are you going to burn rubber on the way out of here? What's that called?" Matt asked, talking fast.

"It's called peeling out and I'm not doing it. It's bad for the car."

"I bet it's because you can't do it."

And he said it with just enough confidence—and she was just annoyed enough—that she revved the engine, peeled out perfectly onto the road, and took off without ever realizing he had never answered her question... so she had no idea where he lived.

9. Hit or Miss

Ana counted the tickets she had left.

"What do you guys think? Ferris wheel? Scrambler?"

"Mully can't," AJ replied faster than Mully would have liked.

"I can! I just choose not to because I don't feel like it," she said.

"Anyone else hungry?" Trin asked.

Mully hit her arm, an instinctual reaction of pure relief which Trin was very used to after four years of drama club. "I'll go with you while those two go on a ride. Ok with everyone?" Mully asked.

AJ scowled. "It's your last night. I don't want to keep splitting up."

"Me either," Ana said, but she was drowned out by Mully sighing in her most over-dramatic tone.

"Could everyone stop saying that like the world is going to end tomorrow?" Mully pleaded.

"Excuse us for missing you," AJ said.

"I'm not gone yet!" she burst out in reply.

Even though he towered over the three of them, AJ seemed to shrink as he stammered out, "But it's only... fourteen hours until you leave. And then Ana goes three hours after that."

There was something about the way he was standing, the way he turned red when Trin said, "Aren't you leaving at the same time?" that tipped them off to something being wrong.

"No, uh, well..." he trailed off.

Mully mustered her most serious voice, low and dangerously quiet. "AJ?" He looked like a kid whose mom had just used his middle name, but he was saved from answering by Ana.

"Are you not leaving tomorrow?" she exploded. "Damn it, you know I'm nervous about being in the city on my own. You said you'd be there every night."

"No, uh, w—"

"Do not say *well* again," Ana snapped.

"It turns out that it's more complicated than that," AJ stammered out.

Ana had a dangerous voice too, and the ice that blasted from her was felt by everyone in a ten-foot radius. "Try me."

"It, um, turns out, well—" he swallowed nervously but she didn't say anything. He looked at the three women staring silently at him and swallowed again before saying, "I can't."

Ana stared at him, blinked a couple times in confusion, then asked, "Can't what?"

Trin's mouth hung open as she looked back and forth between the two of them.

"I can't... go... with you... tomorrow." Each word sounded like it was being ripped one at a time out of the depths of AJ's body as he tried to answer her.

"Fine, then when ARE you coming?" Ana asked as she rolled her eyes in frustration.

"No, I'm not going... I didn't say that right. I can't go to, uh, New York. At all. I can't go."

"But you..." Mully could read how scared AJ was, but she didn't understand what was going on. "You got in," she continued softly, as if talking to herself. "I saw the acceptance letter. You got four acceptance letters and NYU was definitely one of them."

Ana nodded her head automatically.

"Yeah but," AJ couldn't look at any of them. "Just because they let you in doesn't mean you have to go."

"Have to?" Mully prompted.

"Yeah, I—" AJ squared his shoulders and stood up a little taller. "I decided. I'm not going to college."

There was a long pause before Ana let out the tiniest whisper of a swear.

"Fuck." Ana shook herself as if trying to shake off what he had just said before asking at a normal volume, "And when did you decide that?"

AJ deflated again.

"At graduation?"

With no warning, before anyone could even blink, Ana launched herself at AJ and began punching him.

"You bastard! You son of a bitch!" she yelled as he fell to his knees underneath her.

Several people stopped and looked as if they were thinking of intervening as AJ tried to curl up into a little ball to avoid the worst of her blows, but Ana didn't need to be pulled off him. As soon as he was in the dirt, she stopped hitting him. Her chest heaved with effort and she sounded like she was about to start crying, but she kept shouting at him instead.

"You're leaving me alone! I told you—This was all your idea and I went along with it and then I got in and now I'm going and—"

She let out a gasp that was almost a sob and she started hitting him again.

"I'm going and you're staying HERE and you've known this for two months and didn't say a word about it to me?"

At last, her arms fell weakly by her sides but AJ didn't dare move.

"I'm sorry," he said when she remained silent.

"You'll be more than sorry!" she gasped as the tears started escaping down her face.

"You'll be dead," Mully muttered. She wasn't even aware she had said it out loud until Ana whirled around and screamed " *What?* "into her face.

"Sorry, I didn't mean to say anything," Mully said, unconsciously taking half a step backward. "Please, please continue beating some sense into him."

"Did she know?" Ana tossed over her shoulder to AJ, while still glaring at Mully.

He carefully lifted his head maybe one inch out of his hands.

"Um, I'm right here," Mully said to Ana, risking her life.

"She didn't know," AJ said, pushing up onto his feet.

"Yeah, right," Ana spat out.

"He just told you," Mully said, annoyed that Ana was still in her face. But then, without even realizing she was doing it, Mully looked past Ana and over to AJ. She had only meant to catch his eye, make sure he was okay, maybe somehow ask with her eyes if he was telling the truth because how could he have kept a secret like this... But of course all Ana saw was that Mully looked over to AJ, and Mully immediately knew she had made a mistake.

Ana used the back of her hand to roughly wipe her face; she'd stopped crying, and now she took a deep breath before speaking again. "You two are, are—you two are like peas in a pod and you deserve each other. I tried."

AJ began to get up but froze when Ana's icy glare fell on him again. She shook her head. "Don't worry, I'm done hitting you. I'm done with you, period. I tried for four years and I give up, ok?" She looked back at Mully and took a step away before adding, "He's yours to deal with. Good fucking luck."

Ana turned around and walked off. Just walked off into the crowd. Didn't look back, didn't say another word to any of them.

Trin closed her mouth. Mully walked over and stood over AJ, still crouched on the ground. She waited for him to stand up fully and brush the dirt off his pants before saying anything.

"Are you going to go after her?" she asked.

AJ scanned the crowd. He looked down at Mully, rolled his shoulders, grimacing in pain, and answered, "No."

"So what now?" Trin asked.

AJ walked away in the opposite direction from Ana.

Trin and Mully shared a look. A "*what the fuck is wrong with these people*" look, but Mully shrugged and chased off after AJ, leaving Trin alone once again.

Mully grunted in frustration as she tried to squeeze past a group of people by the water gun race booth. She had lost AJ in the crowd, but she knew where to find him.

It was no surprise to see him leaning against the passenger side of her car in the parking lot. It was colder out of the press of the crowd, and so quiet here that she could hear all the crickets going nuts.

She didn't say a word as she walked over and unlocked her driver's side door. She sat down, thought for a moment, and let herself have the satisfaction of slamming the door shut. Then she looked over to see AJ watching her through the passenger window. They looked at each other for a long time—she hoped long enough for him to worry she wouldn't let him in—but finally she leaned over and unlocked the door. He climbed in.

"Well," she said as he put on his seat belt. "This is interesting news to get when I'll be on a plane in the morning. *Thanks.*"

"I wanted to tell you."

He didn't go on, so Mully gave him a wide-eyed stare meant for someone who had obviously lost their mind.

"You've known since graduation?" she said after it was clear he wasn't going to continue. "In two months you never once thought, 'Hey, this would be a good moment to let my best friend in the entire world know that my life has come crashing down around me?'"

AJ leaned forward, straining the seatbelt as he protested, "My life has not come crashing down around me!"

"No?"

"Plenty of people don't go to college," AJ said, slumping back into his seat. He perked up a bit as he added, "Plenty of directors don't even go to college!"

"No, plenty of directors don't FINISH college," Mully said. "They still go, take a couple classes, that sort of thing."

"That can't be true," AJ said sadly, and Mully could tell what she said had gotten through to him at least a little.

"I don't care that you're not going to NYU," she said.

"You make one person in the universe," he replied.

"Ha!" She turned to face him full on. "So you admit you care that you're not going to NYU."

AJ stared straight ahead, not meeting her eyes. "I want

to go. But there's no money for it." He took a deep breath. "That's what I found out at graduation. My dad said one son lazing around the house was bad enough, and he wasn't going to pay for a second one. I couldn't make the money for a place like NYU over the summer. So... I... can't go."

"No wonder you want to kill Jack."

AJ tipped his head back against the headrest and closed his eyes. "I won't kill him..."

"You hoping Ellen will do it for you?" Mully teased.

"I don't want to talk about our siblings," he said, his eyes still shut.

"O...k..."

"Or tomorrow," he snapped.

"Ok," she said, a hint of annoyance creeping into her voice.

He opened his eyes and scowled out the window. Mully played with her keys. The silence in the car was deafening.

"I guess I'm single now," he said casually, as if they had been having a normal conversation.

"Feel weird?" Mully couldn't help asking.

He wrinkled his nose. "A bit."

Mully bit her lip. She had no idea what to say.

"Do you hate me now?" he asked quietly.

"A bit." She smiled to show she was joking. "No, I don't hate you. I'm worried about you."

"Don't be."

"I am."

AJ started to jiggle his leg. "Can we get out of here?"

Mully started to reach her key toward the ignition and hesitated. "Where?"

"Anywhere but here."

"I can do that," Mully said and started the engine.

She turned her key and AJ chose the music in a fluid dance the two of them had performed countless times before. Mully had thought they'd talk more, but he started singing along and she decided to let it go for now.

10. You Learn

Norford High School was a long and low brick building. A covered walkway ran almost the entire length of the front of the building, and two small steps led up to it. Trin shuffled along them, hopping up and down between the two levels as she made her way out of the carnival and toward her car in the far parking lot. Her jeans caught on her heel and she only just managed to stop herself from falling flat on her ass on the sidewalk. She laughed at herself and walked along normally now, pulling her keys out of her bag and jingling them in her hand—and then she remembered.

She looked down at her key ring. Mully had given her keys to the school. She looked up at the dark building and bit her lip. It wouldn't hurt to just *try* the key to the music hallway and see if it even still worked.

She tried to look confident as she walked around the side of the school and let herself into the side door. The key turned without any effort. Trin strolled through the empty hallways, passing through the pools of light and shadow and marveling at how big the building seemed with no one else in it. As she walked by the closed classroom doors, the bright lights of the carnival flashed across her peripheral vision through the small rectangles of window. She listened to the music that echoed from bouncing off the tile floors—someone, somewhere, must have left a window open for it to sound so clear, she thought.

Trin's old locker was in the hallway next to the auditorium, of course, and she looked at it for a minute before reaching out and taking the lock in her hand. It had only been two months since she thought she had closed it for the last time. She would know the combination until she died, she was sure of it, but as she twirled the lock's dial to 13, then 22, then 15, nothing happened.

Trin tugged on the lock, almost panicking, but after a moment she let go and stepped back. The lock swung back against the metal and she had to resist the urge to laugh. They had changed the locks. Of course they changed the locks. Shaking her head at herself, she ventured further into the school.

Most of the administration offices were clustered in one hallway lined with glass walls instead of lockers. The guidance counselor's office had taken advantage of the glass to hang paper ribbons of where every member of the senior class of 2000 had gotten into college all along the hallway. Trin's eyes were drawn to her ribbon as if it were a magnet: Quinnipiac College, University of Connecticut, Willer College. There was a star next to Willer. She wondered who wrote out the ribbons in that flowery script every spring. Then she wondered how long it would be until they took these down. She racked her brain; she had spent four years here, she *must* have seen when they took down the ribbons... But she drew a complete blank.

Trin's ribbon, like her locker, was next to Ana's. Ana Foster: Boston University, Emerson College, *New York University, Simmons College, Univ. of Massachusetts Amherst, Willer College, University of Pennsylvania. The last listing was in a slightly different writing—the same script, but as if the writer had been a little rushed and used a different pen. Trin hadn't thought to wonder before what would have happened if Ana had just gotten into UPenn instead of being waitlisted, but now all the possibilities flew through her mind at warp speed. Would Ana's dad have insisted she go there instead of NYU? Would she have *wanted* to go there instead of NYU? Even without AJ? Because now...

AJ and Mully's ribbons were of course next to each other: one row up and slightly over from Trin and Ana. Adam Cadwallyn: Boston University, Emerson College, *New York University, Univ. of Southern California. Josephine Carr: New York University, UCLA, *Univ. of Southern California. Only Mully could have used UCLA as a safety school. As it was, the guidance counselor had had to beg her to apply to multiple places.

Trin didn't even need to look at the other ribbons to know Mully and AJ were the only people with the word "California" on their ribbons. Most of the others looked more like hers: a mix of Connecticut, New York, and Massachusetts. A couple people going to Brown. One guy was convinced his life would really begin once he arrived at Dartmouth. A handful of people were moving out to Chicago. She let her head sink forward against the nice cool glass, thinking. She closed her eyes and tried to block out the distant sounds of the carnival. She was never getting out of here.

"Do I want to know?" a voice said behind her, and Trin jumped about a mile into the air.

"I was just looking!" she shouted at Mr. Mirana, accidentally raising her voice much higher than intended.

The English teacher and drama club director laughed. He was a short, slim man with dark hair, an easy smile, and a soft spot for his tech crew students.

"It's ok. You're not in trouble." Mr. Mirana put his

hands up in a show of innocence.

"I'm not?" Trin didn't know if he knew about Mully's keys, but she was sure she wasn't allowed to be in here.

"Of course not. I'm sure you're here for a perfectly reasonable reason and gained access to the school through totally legal means," he said quickly.

"Huh?"

"Did you break and enter?" he tried instead.

Trin thought about it before answering, "No. No, I broke nothing."

Mr. Mirana smiled. "Ok then."

"Thanks."

Mr. Mirana had his hands in his pockets, and Trin unconsciously copied him.

"So... why are you here?" she asked.

"Came for the carnival, got nostalgic for the auditorium," he said, shrugging.

She snickered.

"Don't look so surprised. I'm going to miss you guys."

"We tried to leave you a good crew," Trin said.

"Yeah," he sighed, "but I've been very spoiled the past four years."

"I guess it will be weird to have a stage manager other than Mully," she said, unable to meet his eye and gazing intently at the floor.

He took a moment before responding. "And you, too. How many people could go from a techie to running the lights to actress in just one year? And then help manage the next?"

She blushed and stared even harder at the floor. He took his hands out of his pockets and opened his mouth to say something, but she suddenly reached over and tapped the glass over her ribbon.

"I'm going to Willer."

"Good school," he said.

"I don't know what I want to do," Trin said to the glass more than to him.

"Do you need to know right now?"

That got Trin to turn and look at him. Mr. Mirana seemed genuinely surprised at her distress and she tried to explain. "I mean, I have *no* idea what I want to do."

"So?" He went on before she could try to respond. "You've always been able to do anything and everything you've tried."

"That's not a major," she said, shaking her head sadly as if he were missing something.

Mr. Mirana suppressed a laugh, and seemed to be thinking of the best thing to say. He finally said, "It's not a major, but it is better training for life. You don't have to know your major the first week of college. You'll figure it out. Over time. Eventually."

"I guess." Trin looked back at all the college ribbons.

He shook his head almost imperceptibly. "Well, if you're going to be around this year, let me know if you'd like to help out here."

"Help?" Trin wasn't sure how *she* could help *him.*

"I could always use another grown-up. Keep these kids in line. You know how actors are."

"Thanks," Trin allowed herself the smallest smile. "I'll keep that in mind."

"Well, enjoy your evening. I suppose I should get back out there." Mr. Mirana put his hands back in his pockets and started to walk away. "See you around, Trin!" he called over his shoulder.

Trin had been battling to keep it inside but it didn't

seem fair to not let Mr. Mirana know the truth when he'd always been so nice to them.

"AJ's staying too," she shouted after him.

Mr. Mirana spun around and walked backwards without missing a beat.

"But I didn't ask AJ," he said, then spun back around and disappeared into the darkness of the hallway.

Trin stood stunned. He didn't want AJ instead? But AJ was so much more talented than her... She shook her head. Maybe Mr. Mirana needed time to process. She took one last look at the ribbons, then walked off down the hallway in the opposite direction from Mr. Mirana. She didn't have any destination in mind, just wanted to wander.

She was walking through the darkened hallway, listening to the strains of an Alanis Morissette song drifting in from outside, then turned a corner and collided full on with someone.

A very undignified "Oomph!" exploded out of Trin as she staggered a couple feet backwards. But the boy was whispering "Shit! Shit! Shit" as he scrambled to pick up the lacrosse balls that had scattered when he dropped his bag. Trin stood blinking stupidly at Will Thomas—one of the most popular boys in school, a three-season varsity athlete, prom king—until one of the balls rolled into her foot. She stooped to pick it up and held it out.

"Thanks," he said. "Sorry about running into you like that," he added with a nervous smile. She smiled nervously back. Will Thomas was basically her total opposite, but he had always seemed really nice, and she knew he wasn't one of the jerky jocks.

"Yeah, sorry," Trin managed to mumble. She helped him gather up the last few balls and he frowned as he held up the bag and felt its weight in his hand.

"Pretty sure I'm missing some," he said, looking hopelessly at the dark shadows farther along the hallway. "Oh well." He seemed to take in Trin for the first time. "How'd you get in here?"

"Keys from drama club. You?"

"Borrowed some off the team manager. I came in through the boys' locker room."

"Mine smell better," she quipped and then almost bit herself closing her mouth. *Where had that come from?*

But Will was laughing. Trin felt her mouth fall open in shock as she realized he wasn't laughing at her: he was actually amused by her joke.

"Man, I really thought I was busted, running into a teacher," he said, shaking his head.

"What could a teacher do to you now?" she asked.

"Take away the keys?" Will shrugged.

Trin shrugged back. "I wouldn't worry about it. So why are you in here?"

"I came in to get these." He lifted up the dirty canvas bag of lacrosse balls again, then continued, "But coming out of the gym, I saw Mr. Mirana walking around and got scared about getting caught, so I was trying to be quiet."

"You succeeded." Trin smiled at him.

"Yeah, back at you. What are you, a ninja?"

"This side's clear now," she said, ignoring his question. "No one's over here."

"Other than you."

She shook her head. "I don't count."

"Well, jeez, what a thing to say," he sputtered, shaking his head in a mirror image of her. When an awkward silence fell between them, he started walking, and before she could over-think it, Trin fell into step beside him.

"I just meant I'm not a teacher," she said long after the moment had passed.

"It's all good," Will said. He led them outside and around the back of the school in the direction of the sports fields. She could just make out a bunch of kids hanging out on the edge of the football field, some of them tossing a ball around. At this distance, their voices all melded together so that she couldn't make out what any one person was saying.

Will started down the stairs, then noticed Trin still frozen on the top step.

"Are you going to come play?" he asked.

"Huh?"

"We're getting up a game. Four on four," he said. He spoke slowly but there was a patient tone to his voice that made it clear he wasn't annoyed by her confusion.

"A game of what?" Trin felt herself blushing with her own stupidity and was grateful for the darkness.

"Lacrosse," Will said with a sigh. He held up the bag and gently shook it, chuckling.

"Oh, um, I don't play."

"Wait a sec." Will trotted back up the steps so he was right in front of her. "Is there any sport you do play?"

"...No," she said at last.

"So you asked anyway even though no matter what the answer was, you weren't going to come?"

She couldn't tell if he was mad or amused or what but she couldn't bring herself to speak.

"So come on," he said, turning and starting down the stairs again.

"Why?" she called after him.

"Because I'll teach you."

Her head was swimming as she tried to make sense of this conversation. *Why,* after four years of basically never even talking, did Will Thomas suddenly want to hang out with *her?*

"It's night time!" Trin blurted out. Even though it could only have been about 9:30, the sky was dark, and the trees growing around the field made it even darker.

"The white balls show up just fine. Don't worry." Will stopped and looked back to see that she still hadn't moved. "If you're really that nervous, Derek has a glow-in-the-dark ball you can use."

"I can't. I don't know how," she said. She heard the whine in her voice and wished the concrete steps would just open up and swallow her whole. She was blowing it! But surely attempting to play lacrosse and embarrassing herself in front of Will and all his friends would blow it even more, she told herself.

"I just said I'll teach you."

"No, I should get going." Trin felt her car keys in her hand and had no memory of reaching into her bag to get them out. But she didn't want to go away. Her brain was screaming at her legs to just bend and follow this cute guy who wanted to teach her to play lacrosse down the steps, but she couldn't move.

"Where else do you have to be tonight?" Will called up to her.

"I'm sure my friends are looking for me," she lied.

His face fell a little. "Ok." He shrugged. "Well, see you around." And he turned and bounded down the last flight of steps. She turned and walked back to the parking lot so she wouldn't have to watch him join the others and torture herself wondering what he told them about her.

11. I Hope You Dance

Ana pulled into her church's parking lot and turned off the engine. She had intended to drive home and throw herself a pity party all night. The righteous anger had flowed through her as she turned up the radio as loud as she could stand and sang along to Destiny's Child and all the modern pop songs that AJ hated. But she got halfway to her house before realizing that the last thing she wanted to do was explain to her parents why she was home before curfew on a Friday night. She could just see it: her little sisters darting their gaze back and forth between her and the TV, wondering why she had been crying.

And what if her parents wanted to... Ugh! What if her parents wanted to *talk* about it? They had never been huge fans of AJ. Her tall, pale, atheist boyfriend who wrote science fiction and wanted to make movies just hadn't been what they pictured for her. But over the past few years they had finally come to not mind him, and now the last thing she wanted to do was admit that their first instinct had been right.

Plus, if Ana was being totally honest with herself, she didn't want to give her former friends the satisfaction of ruining her last night in her hometown. Right? It was that thought that started the tears again. She had been near her church, so she pulled in and killed her lights. She turned down the radio.

Ana sat in her quiet, dark car, staring at the chain link

fence ahead. She took a couple deep breaths, and was able to stop crying.

Were they really her *former* friends?

Ana looked at herself in the rearview mirror and grimaced. She looked awful. Her eyes were rimmed in red, her face blotchy, and she had no idea how her hair had gotten all out of place. She leaned over and dug a hairbrush out of her glove compartment. As she brushed out the mess on her head, she thought about the carnival. She pictured Mully's face. Mully hadn't known. A little part of Ana's brain kind of wanted her to know; wanted Mully to be some villainess who had conspired with AJ to hurt her. But Mully had been just as surprised. She thought that over. She couldn't think of anything AJ had ever kept secret from Mully. *He must have been so lonely and confused,* she thought before snapping herself out of it. AJ had fucked up, but that didn't make Mully not her friend anymore.

Trin hadn't known either. Trin had done nothing wrong. Trin was still her friend.

Ana threw the brush back in the glove compartment and slammed it shut. It felt good. She looked at her reflection again. Not bad but... She dug into her purse to find her lip gloss. She slathered on ever-so-slightly too much and smiled at herself. She looked human again. She looked like Ana Foster, normal person who could still hang out with Trin and Mully and... and AJ? The smile melted from her face. They all came as part of a set, didn't they?

Ana sighed in frustration. She looked around her car and spotted her Norford High Drama Club sweatshirt in the backseat. It was the softest item of clothing she owned, and she eagerly pulled it over her head. It felt like wearing a warm hug. She fluffed her hair out over the hood. Then without letting herself think any further, she slipped her feet out of her sandals and pulled her legs up onto the seat. She pulled the sweatshirt over them so that her whole body was wrapped up in her hoodie. She hugged her knees and let her head fall against them.

"Let's slow things down," the damn DJ on the radio was saying, and a country song she hadn't heard before came on. It was slow and hopeful and it made tears come to her eyes again, but this time she didn't feel angry or hopeless like she had before. It felt like she just needed to spend some time sitting here alone and letting herself be sad.

It had only been a few songs, but it felt like hours later that Ana lifted her head and wiped her eyes. She unfolded her legs and put her shoes back on. The radio was playing a commercial so Ana looked over her CD options. She only had the soundtracks to various musicals and couldn't imagine listening to any of those right now. She looked over at her passenger seat: AJ's stupid big binder of CDs was right there.

She pulled the binder into her lap and started flipping through it. *I have nothing in common with him*, she told herself. *How did we even end up dating?* She laughed out loud at herself. *Because YOU asked HIM out.* Well, over. Ana had asked AJ if he wanted to come over to her house to hang out after rehearsal one day in freshman year. Drama had only been going a few weeks; she had recognized him from a couple classes, and figured it was worth a shot. She thought he would be all awkward and shy with a girl, but they had ended up making out in her room that very first evening. Then she had to pretend nothing happened while her mom drove him home! Ana remembered thinking they had really pulled it off, but the very next day her parents gave her a curfew and established rules about doors being open if a boy was in there with her.

Now, of course, she realized that they knew exactly what had happened. Oh well. It was all ancient history.

She looked back at the CDs and picked one. She knew at least one thing: she was going to have to see AJ again to give the binder back. She let herself sit there, eyes closed, enjoying the first song. When it ended, she made up her mind: she wasn't going home. She would hang out, see who was around, and eventually run into AJ and give him his CDs. That was the mature, reasonable thing to do.

She turned on the engine and buckled her seatbelt. Ana drove back toward the Post Road, scanning for cars she recognized. No Mully or Trin, but there were a bunch of other seniors at one of the diners. Her stomach gave a rumble, sealing the deal. Ana turned into the parking lot. Before getting out of the car, she checked her reflection again. The lip gloss had faded to the perfect shine. She stepped out of the car. Wearing the sweatshirt and shorts made her legs look miles long. Ana had to laugh at herself for almost going home tonight. She was "Ana Fucking Foster", and tomorrow she would take on New York City.

12. Happy Meal II

AJ followed Mully into her room and stopped short. The corkboard that dominated a whole wall was empty. He had never seen it cleaned off before. Her dad had installed it to keep her from hanging posters and stuff on her walls, and the last few years she had used it to storyboard and track production on her movies. Now AJ felt like the huge blank expanse of cork was looming over him in some vaguely threatening way. He walked over to the window and started playing with Mully's glow-in-the-dark beaded curtain strands like a distracted cat.

"Cut it out," Mully said without even turning around. She was pulling a suitcase out from under her bed. The bed was a frilly white and gold daybed that didn't match anything else in the room, but she had been using it all her life so it never struck either of them as odd. She started packing, completely ignoring him as she pulled clothes from her dresser drawers.

A chastened AJ plopped himself down in the chair at her desk and spun around a few times. When he saw her shoulders tightening, he stopped. AJ hit a few keys on her computer to stop the Matrix screensaver that was scrolling on the monitor and laughed.

"Really Mully? SETI?"

"What do you care? It's not running on your computer."

"It's just so sad—"

She rounded on him. "You yourself have seen—"

"Whoa, we've been over this! I saw an unidentified flying object. Just because I don't know what it was doesn't mean it was aliens."

"You just admitted we saw a UFO!"

The more exasperated Mully got, the more deadpan AJ got.

"An unidentified. Flying. Object. To two kids in the suburbs. Come on, Mully. You're smarter than this."

"We *saw* it," she insisted. She was frowning down at her hands in frustration, and AJ couldn't help wanting to comfort her.

"I'm not even saying there aren't aliens," he said, leaning back in the chair. "I mean, statistically there probably are. But that's just the problem: by the time the math makes sense that there are aliens, there's almost no chance that they would ever visit earth or that we would be able to communicate with them if they did—"

"*Close*—"

AJ ignored her and kept talking. "—because it's most likely that they're just little bacteria cells or something."

"You have no imagination."

"That's why you're the Mulder and I'm the Scully, Mully," he said with a grin.

She rolled her eyes and went back to packing. She threw the last pile of clothes into her suitcase harder than was necessary, and AJ knew she was over it. He turned back to her desk and grabbed a handful of candy out of the open bag next to her keyboard. He tried to ignore the usual mess, knowing Mully would never forgive him if he started cleaning. Instead, AJ opened her boom box and was pleasantly surprised by the

CD already inside. He turned it on and skipped to his favorite Cardigans song.

"Move over," Mully said, reaching over his shoulder and pulling her yearbook out of a pile. It sent the papers on top of it sliding all over and AJ straightened them up before turning around.

AJ stared at the back of her head as Mully packed the yearbook in her suitcase. He'd known that head through so many different hair colors and he couldn't stop thinking about how tomorrow she'd get on a plane and fly away and he wouldn't know what color her hair was unless she *told* him.

Instead of saying anything like that out loud, AJ let a sneer creep into his voice as he said, "You're bringing your yearbook?"

"Why not?" Mully responded without turning around.

"Why on earth would you want to remember high school?"

"Oh please, it wasn't that bad." She paused for a second, "Besides, I might need names."

"Speaking of names, what's yours out there? You going to stay Mully or go back to calling yourself Josephine Carr?"

She hesitated, then went back to carefully packing her video camera into her backpack. She didn't look at him, talking down to her bags instead.

"Josephine Carr sounds like an old lady."

"You could use Joey like your parents do."

"That was a perfectly respectable name until Katie Holmes showed up," Mully said with a sigh.

"I never liked it," AJ said.

"Well you certainly drove it out of everyone's minds for good."

"Thank god for Chris Carter," he grinned.

Luckily she didn't bother to point out that he didn't believe in god. Instead, she kept looking at her hands as she packed and out of nowhere asked him, "So, what are you going to do?"

"About what?" he said to stall for time.

"What do you think? I mean after I leave tomorrow," Mully said. "I'll be at USC and you'll... be... here. Won't you?"

"Where else would I be?" he said as flippantly as he could muster.

"You know damn well you should be at NYU," she said, finally looking up at him.

"I told you, there isn't anything I can do."

"Do you know how many people in the country—in the world—would give their right arm to get into Tisch?"

"Good luck holding the camera steady," he joked.

"I'm serious damnit. Can't you defer for a year?"

AJ shook his head. "My dad won't change his mind."

"So screw him! But defer, work for a year, save up, take a job, anything!"

She had gotten herself more worked up than she'd meant to and he could see her slightly shaking in frustration as she just stood there. He got up and walked over.

"Mully, it's done. It's over." He picked up the fedora hanging on her bedpost and smiled. It felt good to be looking into her eyes instead of avoiding them. It felt right. "You lost today, kid..." He put the hat on her head. "But that doesn't mean you have to like it."

He had meant it as a joke, but now that he was standing inches in front of her and she was still breathing hard, it didn't seem funny at all. It seemed absolutely serious and she was looking at him in a way that made him wish this night would never end and she would never leave. She was so close to him, he could just lean down and... and kiss her? Sure, sometimes he *wondered* what it would be like to kiss Mully but they had never—

Mully took a step back and took off the hat. The moment passed. She hung the fedora back on her bedpost.

"It doesn't make the cut?" he said, then cleared his throat because it felt like in those few seconds, he had somehow lost his voice.

"I don't know," she said, wrinkling her nose. "Showing up at USC with an Indiana Jones hat? I'd probably be laughed off campus."

AJ picked it up and plunked it on his own head before shoving his hands in his pockets.

"How many movies do you think we used this hat in?"

Mully smiled. "Hundreds."

"What if it's your good luck charm?" he teased.

She came closer again, and AJ felt himself stop breathing.

"If I need that hat, then I don't deserve to be in film school. You should have it." She flicked the brim. "For luck."

Then she froze and his thoughts raced wondering what was going through her head. If she just tipped her head back, then they would be...

But neither of them really wanted that. Did they? Her gaze flicked away from him, as if she had decided something.

"Where we're going, we don't need luck," AJ said to break the tension.

There was a knock on the door. Mully spun back to her suitcase and AJ sat back down at her desk a little too quickly, as if there was something to feel guilty about. *But nothing happened*, he told himself. *Maybe I should just go home*, he thought miserably. But the prospect of home was even more miserable.

"You're up late," Mrs. Carr said as she poked her head in the door.

AJ tried to smile at her as innocently as possible and decided to be grateful she'd broken up whatever weird moment had been building between him and his best friend.

"Sorry if we're too loud," Mully said. She shoved her suitcase over to make room on the bed. Mrs. Carr came into the room, but stayed by the door. She leaned against the jamb and crossed her arms over her old t-shirt. She was still dressed, her hair swept up into a bun, with a pair of reading glasses perched on top of her head.

"You guys are fine," she said. Despite being the type of mom who always got called Mrs. Carr by her daughters' friends, she was a pretty laidback parent. Especially on a weekend night in the summer. "Either of you want anything?" she asked.

"No, thanks," AJ answered.

Mully shook her head.

"Did you see your sister?"

"She was at the carnival. Why?"

"I just like knowing where my children are and that they're safe. Crazy, right?"

"We may go out again," Mully said quickly, and AJ had to bite back a laugh. Mully and Ellen didn't have curfews and they liked to take advantage of that now and then to make sure their parents didn't forget and start expecting them home early.

"Well I assumed that Adam wouldn't live here for the rest of his life. Drive careful."

"I will," Mully answered.

Mrs. Carr turned to leave, but an impish smile crossed

her face and she asked with fake casualness, "How's my car running anyway?"

"Mom! MY car is good," Mully sputtered. "You are totally stealing it back as soon as I leave, aren't you?" She crossed her arms like an upset kid.

"Just to keep it in shape until Christmas of course." Mrs. Carr winked to show her no hard feelings and Mully softened—a little bit. "Do you need another suitcase?" her mom asked.

"No, this plus my bag are good. I'll have my backpack with me too."

"Ok... ok, well, you two don't stay up all night. You've, uh, got a pretty busy day tomorrow."

As she left, AJ said, "Good night Mrs. Carr."

"Good night AJ," she answered.

It was not an accident that she left the door ajar behind her.

"Well look at that," AJ said, beaming.

"What?"

"It took years, but even your parents call me AJ. You're a real trendsetter."

"I'll be more impressed when *your* mother says it," Mully said.

She crossed the room to shut her door, but once the door handle was in her hand, she stopped herself and asked AJ, "You don't want to go home, do you?"

"No way."

"I'm hungry."

AJ held out the bag of chocolate towards her.

"Nah, I want real food. Let's get out of here."

He gestured to her bed. "Shouldn't you finish packing?"

Mully shook her head. "It's not like I need winter clothes or anything. I'm done."

"It doesn't look like a lot," AJ said in a sad, distant tone that sounded nothing like him.

"I packed for a semester, not forever," she snapped. "Come on, put that back into sleep and let's go."

AJ shrugged, set the computer back to the screensaver, and grabbed another handful of candy before following her out into the hallway.

13. She

Ellen felt like she had been driving for hours. She'd instinctively headed for the Post Road after leaving the carnival with Matt, but he still wouldn't tell her where he lived. So then she suggested dropping him off at the diner, saying surely he'd find someone he knew. To her shock, the kid refused. Matt had declared that his biggest hope was that his friends would see him driving around with Ellen Carr. It had stopped being quite so flattering, but since Ellen wasn't willing to just ditch him on the side of the road, she was stuck. And once Matt had realized she wasn't going to throw him out of the car, he started talking. And talking. And talking. They were stopped at a red light and she peered up through her windshield at it in disgust. Her favorite Green Day song was playing on the radio but it couldn't compete with whatever the hell Matt was going on about now.

"...but I'm not a fan of Zip Mode because you miss some pretty major stuff. I mean, sure, you get through the game, but that isn't the point, duh. And *Riven* is so much harder to begin with, you need all the clues you can get. But the graphics! Oh man, I mean, you knew it was going to be good when they were developing it, and it's a huge step up, but it's just a whole other level..."

"Jesus, don't you ever shut up?" she finally snapped at him.

Then, three things happened simultaneously. Matt

opened his mouth to respond; the light turned green; and police lights came on from the car behind them.   Ellen sighed and cleared the intersection before pulling over to the side of the road. She turned down the radio and slumped back in her seat.

Matt's mouth was still hanging open and his eyes were wide. "What's going on?" he whispered.

"Don't worry about it," Ellen said. "Just keep your mouth shut."

He closed his mouth.

Ellen's window was already rolled down as the cop walked up to them. He was older than Ellen by only a couple years, and walked so slowly that it seemed to take forever for him to cover the short distance between their cars. Then he leaned down and rested his forearms on her open window in a way that certainly would have gotten him written up if he had done it to anyone else's car.

"Ellen Carr," the cop said with a grin.

"Officer Switt," she deadpanned, staring straight ahead.

"I like the sound of that." He looked around the car. "You're not going to be out all night causing trouble, are you?"

"Jason, I wasn't doing anything wrong. I'm just going home from the carnival, giving my friend here a ride."

Matt smiled, trying to look helpful. Switt ignored him.

"Jason? No, that's not quite the same, is it?" he said, letting the corners of his mouth droop.

Ellen swallowed her pride. "Officer."

"Your car's pretty distinctive," he said, letting his eyes roam over each inch of its exterior before leaning back into Ellen's window, a little closer to her this time.

"That's not a crime," she said, still staring ahead at the road.

"I'd be willing to bet you and your dad have made some modifications," he said slowly.

"Do you want to see the registration?" Ellen asked, the slightest tinge of irritation creeping into her voice.

"No, no," Switt grinned at her again. "I just wanted to give you a little advice: Go home, stay home. You and Jack Cadwallyn may think you're invincible but it'll end badly for you two."

Ellen bit out her words rather than give in to how angry his condescending tone made her. "Jack? Jack and I barely know each other. Our families are friends, but if he's stupid enough to race, that's his business, not mine."

"You forget, I helped clean up that wreck. I saw—"

"I already told—"

"Could I have seen lights on the underside?" The cocky lilt in his voice was back. "Not street legal, things like that."

"I would never be so tacky as to put lights on the underside of my car!" Ellen shouted, then reeled herself back in. Jason was a cop now, and she continued in a much calmer tone as she explained, "Anyway, from what I hear, Jack's driving his mother's station wagon these days."

Jason looked from Ellen to Matt one more time before nodding and walking away without any further explanation. He got in his patrol car, turned off the lights, and pulled smoothly back onto the Post Road.

Ellen took a moment to collect herself. She put her hands at ten and two and made herself take two deep breaths in through the nose and out through the mouth before putting the car into drive and pulling back onto the road.

They drove three blocks before Matt couldn't take it anymore. "What the hell?" he exploded.

"Cops can pull you over for no reason at all," Ellen replied, shrugging in resignation.

"But he—"

"He's an ex and an asshole," she said quickly.

Matt digested this bit of information.

"His name's Switt?" he finally asked.

"Jason Switt."

"Officer Switt..." Matt smiled. "You can do a lot with that name."

"Yeah, you can. But honest Matt, it's better to just keep your mouth shut. Don't feed the fire."

"If you say so. I still think it sucks dead donkey balls. Do you really race cars? Like he said? I mean, you said this one was really fast."

Ellen laughed. "Do you see any straight streets around here other than the Post Road?"

"No," Matt admitted.

"And it has about seven million cops watching it. So no racing."

"But he said—"

"Damn," Ellen frowned, ignoring him.

"What now?" Matt swung his head around, eyes wide.

"I've been driving around and not paying attention and we need gas. We'll stop first then I'll take you home."

"Oh yeah," Matt said.

She smiled and watched him out of the corner of her eye. "You forgot you were just going home, didn't you?"

"Didn't you?" he asked back.

He was right: she had forgotten. Ellen stopped smiling.

14. The Impression That I Got

Trin pulled into a gas station and took note of the pump number as she got out. This one didn't have a credit card option at the pump, so she ran under the awful fluorescent lighting into the store to pay. When she came out, Trin pressed the button for regular and used the nozzle to flip up the holder. She set the pump and leaned against her car, feeling at peace as she listened to the gas pouring into her tank. She recognized the song playing softly through the station's speakers, and she started singing along.

Ellen's car pulled up to the pump behind Trin's. Ellen got out, and a boy Trin didn't recognize came out of the passenger seat. Ellen gave him a twenty to pay inside.

"Premium on 3!" she yelled after him.

Trin knew Ellen had spotted her. It was pretty much impossible not to recognize her blue hair and equally bright blue car. Once Ellen had inserted the pump and set the placeholder to pump for her, she came over to say hi.

"How's it going?" Ellen said.

"It goes," Trin said. "Who's that?"

"Laddie's brother," Ellen said with a shrug.

Trin debated asking who on earth Laddie was, but she chickened out and hummed a few notes along to the music instead.

"So you guys gave up on the carnival too?" Ellen asked.

"Yeah. I mean, it's probably almost over anyway. They

don't go as late anymore."

Ellen laughed. "I'll bet they go the same amount of time, but it doesn't feel as late when you're not a little kid."

"Good point. So, what are you and... Laddie's brother up to?"

"Just driving."

"Cool," Trin said.

They lapsed back into silence but it only lasted a moment before Ellen blurted, "Hey, have you seen AJ's brother tonight?"

"No, why?"

"No real reason." But Ellen looked worried.

Ellen's pump clicked off and she went back over. She frowned at the pump, took the nozzle, and hand pumped it to get all her money's worth.

The kid came out of the station and Trin took a closer look to see if she recognized him. The first thing her brain registered was that it looked like he had a cigarette dangling from his mouth, and she did a double-take before realizing it was actually the stick from a Fun Dip packet.

"You're not eating that in my car," Ellen snapped at him as she opened her door.

"Fine," the boy said, and defiantly ripped open the sugar packet. He stopped, tipped his head back, and ate the entire thing. He did choke a little bit as he tried to swallow, but it was still pretty impressive.

"You've defeated the point of Fun Dip!" Trin laughed at him.

"You want the other packet?" he asked.

"Well, sure. Thanks."

He broke the stick in half and put the piece that hadn't been in his mouth back in the package before tossing it to her.

Trin just managed to catch it.

"See you around," Ellen said out her window. She started the car as the kid climbed in on his side.

"Sure!" Trin smiled at the two of them as she watched them through the windshield. They were obviously bickering about what to listen to. That was one good thing about being alone in your car, Trin thought. The two of them reached some sort of truce, and Ellen took off into the night.

Trin ripped off the open sugar packet and threw it away before tossing the rest through the open window onto her passenger seat. Then she heard her pump click off. She debated trying to hand pump it to the even dollar amount, but she chickened out. It was only four cents short.

15. Cryin'

AJ hopped out of Mully's Jag as soon as she parked it in the lot next to the Post Road Diner. The few spots out front were already full, and besides, Mully loved the mural back here. The entire side of the building had been painted to look like a drive-in during the 1940s or '50s, complete with classic cars and a black-and-white film on the big screen. AJ thought it was cool, but it meant more to Mully because her family had lived in Norford back when the drive-in still existed. AJ looked over his shoulder at her staring at the mural all goony-eyed and smiled in spite of himself. It was cute how even now, bathed in the neon light from the diner's sign so the colors were all slightly off, Mully would stop and imagine her grandparents going on dates here.

"You coming?" AJ gently interrupted.

"Yeah, of course," she said, hurrying to catch up to him.

AJ and Mully entered the chrome mothership of teenagers: the only place in Norford open 24 hours a day. No one cared if the food was actually any good or not or that the owners always left the radio tuned to the classic rock station. By virtue of its offering greasy food any time of day, it was automatically the most popular hang out in town. It was so popular that even the "cool" kids liked it.

Unfortunately.

AJ stiffened as his eyes landed on Ana sitting with Derek and Johnny and all those jerks. It made a sort of sense, since Ana had always gotten along better with more people than they had; she looked perfectly at home talking with the other former seniors there in the booth. But it still felt like a betrayal to see her just... there. In the diner, talking and laughing, as if the carnival had never happened. AJ saw her eyes flick over toward the door, and she must have seen them, but the next thing she did was actually lean *closer* toward Johnny.

"Come on," Mully said, half-shoving AJ onto a stool at the counter. He felt his butt hit the stool and automatically grabbed a menu to hold in front of his face. He studied it intently as if this was the first time he'd even seen such a thing. But the entire time his eyes kept darting around the side to see what Ana was doing.

"Of all the gin joints in all the world?" Mully said.

"Shut up," AJ hissed without even bothering to look at her.

She opened her mouth to say something but AJ was saved by Trin arriving and plopping down onto the stool on Mully's other side.

"Hey!" Mully said, smiling at last. "What are you doing here?"

"Saw your car," Trin said with a grin.

It was all *too* normal, and AJ started to stand up as he said, "We're not staying."

"Yes we are!" Mully used one hand to yank the menu away from him and the other to push him back down onto the stool. She handed the menu to the bored-looking waitress behind the counter. "Fries and a coke please."

"Onion rings," Trin added.

The waitress looked expectantly at AJ.

"Fine!" he hissed at Mully. "Milkshake," he added in the waitress's direction, his eyes already drawn back toward the booths as if Ana were a magnet.

"One fries, one onion rings... you want a water with that?" the young woman asked Trin.

"Yes please," Trin answered.

"And a coke and a milkshake." The waitress looked up at AJ again. "Chocolate?"

"Vanilla."

"Got it," she said, already turning away from them.

"You are the most boring person on earth," Mully informed AJ.

He didn't answer. The group Ana had been with was paying up. They were leaving. They were going to have to walk right past him to get out the door. Despite his attempt to slow down his thumping heart, AJ felt himself start breathing heavily as they grew nearer. He knew he was going to say something, and he opened his mouth without even knowing what would come out of it next.

"Where are your new friends going?" he snarled, and inwardly gave a huge sigh of relief that his voice sounded normal.

Without missing a beat, Ana answered, "We've all known each other our whole lives. Don't be a jerk."

But she stopped walking. AJ leaned back against the counter. She crossed her arms. He crossed *his* arms. After a moment of staring at each other, AJ jerked his head toward the empty stool next to him, and Ana sat down.

"Oh for..." he heard Mully mutter.

AJ fought to keep from shaking as he stared at Ana. Even though he had been the one to invite her to sit down, he hadn't actually thought she would! Why would she join them? Had she forgiven him? What did it mean if Ana was sitting mere inches away from him now?

"You left your CDs in my car," Ana said casually. Then she looked past him to Mully and Trin, and he desperately tried to think of something to say.

The awkward silence was broken by the waitress arriving with their food.

"That looks really good," Ana said. "Can I get a vanilla milkshake too please?" she asked the waitress.

AJ concentrated on opening his straw. It was something he'd done a million times, but now that he was thinking about the steps involved, he had become totally paranoid that he'd do it wrong.

Mully snickered next to him and said, "Most. Boring. People. Ever." He resisted the urge to push her off her stool.

Out of the corner of his eye, AJ saw Ana make a face at Mully. Then she reached across him to steal a French fry from Mully's plate. Her arm was so close to his face that AJ instinctively reared back and basically stopped breathing.

"Thief, thief, thief!" Mully playfully smacked Ana's hand, but let her grab a handful of fries.

AJ was sure he had passed out, turned invisible, or s*omething* as the girls around him started talking like it was any other Friday night.

"So where we going next?" Ana asked.

"The river?" Trin suggested.

"The river blows," Mully dismissed the idea out of hand.

"Derek's having a party," Ana said. "I'm sure no one will say anything if we just show up."

"Derek?" AJ's brows could not have furrowed any

more.

"They got a keg from Vista. He seemed pretty psyched," was all Ana answered. She narrowed her eyes at him, and AJ felt the waves of ice coming off her as if they were a physical force.

"Can't we just hang out at your house?" Mully asked.

Ana snorted. "And watch *The Matrix* for the seven millionth time? No thanks."

"Or *Star Wars*," Mully suggested.

"Or *Raiders*," AJ said tentatively, ready to retreat into a ball if Ana decided to hit him.

"Or—" Trin started to say, but Ana cut her off.

"Or not," Ana said quickly, but she was smiling. And not hitting AJ, which was a huge relief no matter how this night ended up going. In fact, Ana shook her head and laughed as she added, "I can't wait for you losers to see *Lord of the Rings*."

"I can't wait to see this dwarf Bilbo that your cat is named after," Mully said.

"He's a hobbit, not a dwarf! I mean," Ana seemed to catch herself nerding out and continued more quietly, "Just trust me, you'll get it once you see it. He IS a total Bilbo. Which you'd already know if you'd read the books like I suggested."

AJ snorted into his milkshake. "That book is so boring I couldn't even finish it."

"Books," Ana blurted, emphasizing the S, but he didn't register the correction.

"Nothing happens," he declared.

"Nothing hap—Nothing happens?!" The color drained out of Ana's face. "You people are so uncultured. Gandalf, Aragorn, every horse and sword has a name! You love shit like that. And these films are going to be amazing." She continued on as if she were trying to convince herself. "If they're good. But they should be good. I hear good things. The director is, like, obsessed."

AJ stared blankly at her. God, he loved her when she got like this.

"Well, it's filming in Australia, so that's a good sign," Mully said, snapping him back to the present moment.

"New Zealand," Ana corrected with a sigh.

"Same thing," Mully said.

Ana stared at the three of them in disgust. Finally, Trin mustered up, "Hobbit... isn't that a book too?"

"You all suck," Ana announced. But before she could elaborate, the waitress delivered her milkshake. AJ watched her unwrap her straw (no trouble there that he could see) and close her eyes as she took the first cold sip. Her forehead scrunched up for a moment as the sugar rush hit, then Ana opened her eyes and for just a moment looked at him.

He knew with every cell in his body that this was the moment to say something. To apologize for not telling her everything back in June, for being so chicken-shit all summer, for leaving her to go to New York City alone. To say that he didn't want to be broken up, even though he understood why she had done it. To ask if she still loved him, to offer to try to read Tolkien again, anything!

"Pass me the ketchup," Mully demanded, and AJ broke eye contact with Ana to find the bottle and slide it over.

When he looked back at Ana, she was staring straight ahead at the wall behind the diner counter. He telepathically tried to will her to look at him again, but obviously his chance had passed. Mully and Trin dumped their plates together into a massive pile of fried deliciousness to share, and AJ forced himself to look away from Ana and ask them for an onion ring and pretend everything was normal.

16. What's the Frequency, Kenneth?

Jack Cadwallyn pulled into the diner's parking lot and parked out front, away from the mural. He looked exactly like what he was: an older version of his brother AJ. Same brown hair, same blue eyes, same height that somehow made them seem a little arrogant, when really, they were just tall. Unlike AJ though, Jack had always been a prep at heart and tended to wear khakis and button-down shirts. When they'd been at Willer together, Ellen had always teased him that he dressed like their professors. No one had made that comparison since she went back to school and Jack stayed home though. A favorite song of his was just starting on the radio, and he let himself sit for a little longer so he could drum along on his dashboard.

It was a good dashboard, no matter what some people thought. The gray 1995 Ford Taurus station wagon had been meant for his mother, but since his father had made him wait until he was eighteen to get his license, his mom had always been nice about letting Jack drive it whenever he wanted. Their dog liked to sit in the passenger seat and put his paws up on the dash, so there were several deep gashes in the plastic. Jack ran his hand over them, a smile playing across his face, then turned off the engine.

He got out and leaned against his car, waiting for someone to walk by. It only took a couple minutes before a whole group of kids came out of the diner and, lucky him, the two stragglers on the steps were a couple of cute girls. Too young for him, really, but not so young that a little flirting wouldn't work. He hoped.

"Hey, is Ellen Carr in there?" he called to them.

"Me? Hi. Hello, um, Jack. Hi, I'm Megan," the braver one stammered as they walked over. The neon lights of the diner's sign bounced off the glitter around their eyes. Even before they reached him, Jack could faintly smell Tommy Girl. The contrast between a scent he knew so well and their shiny make-up made it hard for him to judge their age, but if they knew who he was, they must be at least high school seniors.

"Hi Megan." He gave her his best smile but couldn't be distracted. "You seen Ellen?"

"No. But she was at the carnival earlier."

"She's driving around?"

"Probably," said the other girl. "Come on Megan," she hissed as she pulled Megan's arm toward the car.

Jack didn't let his smile drop—part of being charming was not minding that not every girl fell for his charm.

"Her sister's inside with AJ and that girl Trin," Megan said despite her friend's yanking.

"Thanks hun, but I'm not looking for them." He winked for good measure, and turned to get into his car.

"He's too old for you," he heard the friend hiss at Megan.

Jack turned around. "Trin? Blue hair?"

"Yeah," Megan managed to stand her ground for a moment.

"What's a girl like that doing with losers like my brother?" Jack asked, then swung himself down into his driver's seat.

Megan stood stunned for a moment, then gave in and ran over to her friends already piled into a brand-new mint green VW Beetle.

"I can't believe he talked to you!" the driver howled with glee as Megan got in.

With as much of a roar as a station wagon can muster, Jack took off in a long silver streak into the night.

17. Out Tonight

Ana, AJ, Mully, and Trin tumbled out the door of the diner and down the front steps to the parking lot.

"We never decided what to do," Trin pointed out.

"That's because you sidetracked me with your ludicrous theories like *Crusade* being better than *Raiders*," Mully shot back.

"We could drive around for a while. Just hang out. It's still early enough," Ana suggested quietly. Other than the awkwardness of not talking to AJ, hanging out in the diner with them had felt normal enough. And normally what they would do next is pile into a car and sing along to the radio for hours. "AJ, you still need your CDs anyway. I could drive. For a while," she added.

"Awesome idea," Trin said, nodding overenthusiastically in encouragement. Ana shot her a look of gratitude.

Then she steeled up all her courage and made herself look at AJ.

"Sounds good," he shrugged.

They headed over to Ana's car and as she was unlocking the doors, Mully stopped and out of nowhere said, "Be right back."

Ana's first instinct was to be annoyed but then she realized Mully was running over to her own car, probably to grab something she needed.

It wasn't until she was sitting in her seat that Ana realized AJ had automatically taken shotgun and was right next to her in the front. She frantically tried to think if this *meant* anything as she slowly clicked on her seatbelt, but her logical brain told her that it was just habit. She tried to take a deep breath without him or Trin noticing. Thank god Trin was busy clearing off the rest of the backseat for Mully by pushing everything down onto the floor, and AJ had grabbed his CD binder and was flipping through it. Ana forced herself to shake it off. AJ was in her car. AJ looked good. She closed her eyes for a quick second, then forced herself to open them and continue with her thoughts. AJ was her ex-boyfriend now, and if she wanted to hang out with her friends tonight instead of going home and crying into a carton of ice cream, she needed to act like everything was fine.

Mully pulled a warm flannel shirt on over her Star Wars t-shirt as she hurried back from the Jag, her Doc Martens thudding across the parking lot. As soon as she landed in the backseat and closed the door, Ana threw her car in reverse and pulled out of the parking lot onto the Post Road.

Ana was an aggressive driver, going fast on any straight-a-ways but rougher on the curves than Mully was. As usual, she ignored the image of Mully in her rearview mirror, staring out the window with her jaw clenched. Mully had once offered to give Ana driving lessons and they hadn't spoken for a week afterwards. It had never been mentioned since.

Out of the corner of her eye, Ana saw AJ reach to put on one of his CDs.

"What do you think you're doing?" Ana asked him.

AJ froze. She hadn't even said it particularly meanly, but he still looked like a deer in headlights.

"Music?" he said, holding up the CD.

Ana frowned. She basically only had CDs of cast recordings in her car and knew that the radio tuned to the pop station from New York City wasn't AJ's cup of tea, but still.

"I can change it," she finally said, and AJ unfroze enough to put the CD back in his binder.

Keeping the car steady, Ana put in the soundtrack to *Rent.* She heard AJ's binder thunk as he dropped it at his feet. She smiled as she drove. It felt like she'd passed some sort of test. Mully and Trin were singing their hearts out, and she joined them.

As she changed lanes, Ana caught a glimpse of AJ staring out the window and wondered what *he* was thinking. Maybe he regretted coming with them and would leave as soon as she stopped the car. Maybe he hated her for being able to go to college when he couldn't. Maybe he was still in love with her and would get back together if she just asked?

Ana felt her hands shake a tiny bit on the wheel and missed a note. She could *feel* it as AJ turned away from the window and looked at her instead. She bit her lip, nervous about what he would say.

AJ started singing along.

Maybe, just maybe, Ana felt herself praying, she could just have fun with her best friends from high school for one more night.

Her car full of singing and happiness, Ana turned off the Post Road onto some back roads. The BMW roared underneath the streetlights, twisting and turning along with the asphalt. They were in the neighborhoods near the high school, on roads that they had all gotten to know intimately over the past four years. As they rounded a corner, AJ interrupted their singing to gleefully warn everyone: "Coming up."

All four of them rolled down their windows, hot wind overwhelming the air-conditioned interior. AJ, Mully, and Trin stuck their heads out the windows.

"Three, two, one..." Mully counted down as they drew nearer.

"FUCKER STREET!" they all screamed as they drove past the turn onto Flicker Street. Poor little side road: because it was all capitalized, the sign most definitely, indisputably, clearly read "Fucker St."

They were still laughing as they rolled up their windows. Ana realized it was the perfect moment to show off a teeny bit and said, "Hey, want to see what I figured out the other day?"

"What?" Trin shouted over the music.

"That's a yes," Ana said with a devilish grin. She sped over to the nearest elementary school and pulled into the deserted parking lot. Ana drove down the bus lane and stopped the car.

She turned down the music. "Ok, everyone open your doors."

"What?" Trin asked dubiously.

"Just trust me."

They opened their doors with varying degrees of trepidation.

Ana put the car in reverse and sped backwards down the bus lane as fast as she could.

"Ana..." AJ just had time to start saying before—

Ana slammed on her brakes and screeched to a stop. All four doors slammed shut.

There was a moment of stunned silence.

"Physics!" Ana shouted triumphantly.

Her friends stared at her, mouths agape and eyes

blinking rapidly before they all started laughing and freaking out at once.

"You're a genius!" Trin yelled, slapping the back of Ana's seat.

"Do it again!" Mully begged with a gleam of pure joy in her eyes.

Ana complied. It took them five goes to start tiring of the new trick, at which point Ana drove back toward town.

As they passed the high school, Trin practically lay across Mully's lap to look at the few cars remaining in the parking lot after the carnival ended.

"That's Will's car, right? The red one?"

"It is," Ana said after a quick glance over.

"Why?" AJ asked. He sounded annoyed.

"I just... wondered," Trin said, sitting back up in her seat. Her face was turning beet red.

"You can do better," Mully said at the same time Ana told her, "You'll meet so many guys at college." Ana quickly caught Mully's eye in the rear view mirror, and both girls shut up, embarrassed to be talking to Trin like she was a child just because she'd never had a boyfriend.

Unfortunately, this left a silence in the car that grew more awkward as Ana worked her way back over to the diner. By the time she pulled into the spot next to Mully's car, everyone was just staring out their own window.

Ana turned off the engine and tried not to feel stupid for driving to the diner. She didn't want to go home, but now everyone would get out and leave and... that would be it? She looked at her dashboard as the song changed and instead found herself checking on the clock.

"Hey guys? It's tomorrow," Ana whispered.

"Huh?" Mully asked.

"It's tomorrow. I mean today. It's—it's after midnight," she said, still looking at those little lit-up numbers that said 12:11. "I move to New York City t*oday*."

"Whoa," Trin said softly.

In that moment, something clicked in Ana, because her first instinct was to feel bad that she brought up NYC in front of AJ. But then she realized: she *didn't* feel bad. She was still moving today, even if he wasn't. Ana even felt a little warm glow inside as she finally accepted that AJ had been her high school boyfriend, and he had given her the idea to even apply to NYU, but now she was going to go off on an adventure by herself. Something special that was just for her, not for her as part of a couple or as part of the drama club or part of a friend group. It had been a very, very long time since Ana had experienced anything like that. And it was terrifying and exciting at the same time.

She looked around the car at her three friends. Only Mully would make eye contact. It was like a little electrical current passed between them, and Mully said, "I'm going to keep driving around, if you guys want to stay out."

Ana smiled her thanks. "I've got almost two hours until curfew. I'm in."

18. Breathe

Mully could not bring herself to think of today as being the day she was moving to California. She had to get behind the wheel before her head exploded. Everything would be alright once she was driving.

"Shotgun!" Trin yelled as she slapped the front passenger door of Mully's Jag.

AJ shot Mully a look of horror over the roof of the car, and she shrugged in response. He and Ana would have to figure things out themselves. As Mully put on her seatbelt, she could just see AJ building a little barrier wall in the backseat between him and Ana made up of his CD binder, the tape recorder, and the other flannel shirt that they had left back there. She tried not to laugh, but it was so childish that she did smile a little bit. If Ana really still had a problem with AJ, all she had to do was stop hanging out with them. She'd gotten in the car, so obviously he was safe enough.

There wasn't any plan for where to go or what to do next, so Mully started driving back towards the high school. Even though she couldn't top Ana's earlier door-closing trick, she couldn't resist showing off a little.

"Watch this," Mully said, letting go of the steering wheel and pushing her leg up so her knee could move it as she flew down the side road.

"That's nothing," Trin said with mock bravado. "I could drive this road with my eyes closed!"

"We've all tried that," Mully replied immediately, but she didn't try now because they had all learned the hard way that it was much, much harder than it seemed.

Mully turned onto the road their high school was on, taking the left particularly viciously. A laugh of pure delight escaped her as she sped up when the road straightened out. This was just what she needed.

"What do you think? Should I do it?" she called over her shoulder to AJ.

"Do it. I'll get the music."

"Do what?" Ana said as Mully opened her sunroof. AJ was leaning forward with a CD and frowned at the road ahead of them.

"We don't have enough room now."

Mully used a side road to loop around. AJ had to grip Trin's seat hard to keep from flying around as she took the turns.

"Roll up your window Trin," Mully instructed as she turned back onto the school road.

Trin did, despite the confusion written across her face.

"Physics, right?" Mully said to Ana. "Time for some history."

AJ leaned forward and popped the CD into her Discman. He pressed play, and "Flight of the Valkyries" filled the car as Mully floored it, accelerating to sixty on the straight road. With the sunroof open and everything else shut, the pressure made a noise exactly like a helicopter, and even though it hurt their eardrums, everyone laughed in recognition.

The moment was soon over. Mully had to slow down as the road narrowed and turned twisty again. She and Trin both rolled their windows back down, laughing at each others' crazy hair from the wind.

"Can you put on something else?" Ana shouted through the classical music.

AJ handed a CD to Trin, Trin switched the discs, and Mully was aware that AJ had just started to sit back down when suddenly there were headlights blinding her. She swerved to avoid the car coming toward them and felt the thump against her seat as AJ's body bumped into it. She glanced back only long enough to see that he was fine; he had practically landed in Ana's lap which was embarrassing but not something she could do anything about.

She ignored him trying to mumble an apology to Ana and instead stuck her head out the window. Using every swear word she could think of, Mully let the car know exactly what she thought of them.

"Sorry guys," she apologized in a much quieter tone to her passengers. "They took that curve way too wide," she continued, mostly to herself.

"That scared you, didn't it?" Ana said behind her.

"I'm not scared," Mully tossed over her shoulder. "Just annoyed."

She felt Ana pull herself up to peer over the seat. Mully stopped ever-so-slightly bobbing her head along with the music and asked, "What?"

Ana sat back down and let out a low whistle. "It's just, like, you're not lying."

"*Lying*?" Mully asked.

"A car came way too close, you avoided it, and then you cussed them out. And now it's like it never even happened." Ana paused for half a second, then added, "You should race."

"Where—" Mully started to reply with a roll of her

eyes.

Ana cut her off. "Everyone knows the parking lot at Stanfield High is exactly a quarter of a mile," she said matter-of-factly.

"That's not my style," Mully scoffed.

"I know..." Ana would have to admit that Mully had her there: the idea of Mully drag racing just seemed silly. "But they say people race on Miskwa Hill all the time," she continued stubbornly.

"No one does that anymore," AJ said quickly.

"Sorry for thinking Mully would be amazing," Ana shot at him.

"Miskwa Hill is a dangerous street even on a normal day, and anyone who races on it is an idiot," Mully said as evenly as she could.

"I mean, the 'race' is about 15 miles an hour. But you'd kill it," Ana said, turning back to her.

"That's fast enough," Mully said quietly. She didn't want to be having this conversation, and she felt super awkward that Ana had used the word "kill" but, she had to admit, it was kind of flattering that Ana thought she was that good...

Mully was saved by spotting an unmistakable red car ahead of them. "Hey! That's Ellen."

Trin squinted through the windshield. "She's got someone in the car with her."

"Is it Jack?" AJ asked.

"Not likely," Mully answered.

"I can't tell," Trin said after another moment's study.

Mully unknowingly did a bunch of math in her head and took the risk to swerve into the oncoming traffic lane so she could pull up alongside Ellen's car.

"Hey bitch, what are you up to?" Mully yelled past Trin out her open window.

"None of your business," Ellen said, not even glancing over.

"Hello, who are you?" Mully continued.

"I'm Matt—" the guy in Ellen's passenger seat shouted back eagerly.

"Shut up," Ellen cut him off. "Mully, stop messing around and get behind me."

With a grin, Mully goosed her gas *just* enough to make Ellen think she was going to try to pull in front of her, knowing Ellen couldn't resist speeding up *just* enough to keep her blocked. They kept goading each other—that little bit of back and forth—all the way to the end of the street. Since Mully could see across a couple houses' yards and there was no one else around, she stayed on the wrong side of the road and stopped next to Ellen.

"See? See, that's just what I was talking about," Ana protested from the backseat.

Mully ignored her to yell at Ellen again. "Have a nice date!"

Ellen gave her the finger and Mully double-tapped her horn before turning left and driving down the correct side of the street. Ellen turned right.

19. The Choice is Yours

Matt turned the radio back up as they drove away.

"You should have smoked her!"

"What?" Ellen said.

"You two were totally racing and you could have beaten her," he explained.

"We weren't racing. We were just... messing around."

"But you could have beaten her, right?" Matt persisted.

Ellen allowed herself the teeniest smile of satisfaction. "Maybe I held back a little."

"Could you teach me? When I get my license, I'm going to get the fastest car in Norford and show everybody up."

"Oh, are you?" Ellen teased. "You're going to restore a priceless vehicle and take care of it and then just wrap it around a tree someday?"

Matt's eyes were wide. "That wouldn't—"

"Racing around here is dangerous and anyone who pretends it isn't is kidding themselves," Ellen continued. The teasing note was gone and as she went on, she seemed to be talking more to herself than to Matt. "Half the time the only people willing to risk it are drunk, which makes it even worse. As if it weren't a bad idea to begin with. And then..." she trailed off. Ellen shook herself and bit out, "You can't race a car in Connecticut."

Matt gave her a moment before asking, "So if you

don't race anymore, what do you do every night?"

Ellen sighed. "Usually? Get drunk at someone's house. End up walking home at five in the morning and watch the sun come up."

"What about the river?" he asked.

"It's not like it's any different than drinking in someone's house. Except, oh wait, yes it is, because at someone's house you're warm and not getting bitten by a billion mosquitoes." She laughed.

Matt opened his mouth and Ellen preemptively said, "No, we're not going to the stupid river."

He shut his mouth.

But it was Matt and he couldn't just sit in silence for more than a minute.

"So that was Mully Carr," he said. Ellen didn't respond. Matt added, all in one breath, "I think her going to California is the coolest thing that's ever happened to an NHS grad."

"That's pathetic," Ellen said without thinking.

"You don't think she'll make it as a big Hollywood director?"

"No, I think she will."

Matt had no idea how to respond to that. Ellen didn't elaborate. She never took her eyes off the road as she fished her pack of cigarettes out of her purse, took one out, put it to her lips, returned the pack to her bag, and lit the cigarette. Matt stared at her.

"What? You want one?" she asked as she blew some smoke out her window.

"No."

They drove in silence, until they couldn't resist singing along with the radio, "Engine, engine, number nine, on the

New York transit line..."

They both laughed, and Matt took advantage of the thawed atmosphere to say, "Sorry if I was, like, rude."

"No worries," Ellen said, tapping her ash out the window.

"I've never had one," Matt said. His tone was quiet, as if he were a little bit embarrassed.

Ellen got the pack back out and handed it to him.

He stared at it in his lap instead of looking at her. "I'm not sure I want one."

"Here." Ellen handed him her already-lit cigarette. Matt leaned out his window and inexpertly puffed on it twice before sitting down properly and handing it back to her.

"Not a fan?" Ellen asked.

"My mouth feels gross," he said while making a face.

She rooted around in her bag one-handed again and pulled out a pack of gum.

"Thanks," he said, grabbing the gum with much more enthusiasm than he had taken the smokes.

"No problem," Ellen said. She finished the cigarette and flicked the butt onto the street. "I need to quit anyway."

Matt looked at the mostly-empty pack of cigarettes in one hand and the gum in the other.

"How's that going for you?" he asked as he returned them both to her purse.

"So are you finally going to tell me where you live?" Ellen asked, letting a little irritation creep into her voice to get back at him for that crack. "After all, you've probably still got a curfew you need to make."

"I already missed it," he admitted. Then Matt started speaking very fast. "Hey, are you sure we can't swing by the river before you take me home? We wouldn't have to stay very long. Just to see if anyone I know would see me—I mean, is over there?"

"No," Ellen said flatly.

"Well maybe there are still people at the high school."

"No."

Matt sulked. "I'm not telling you where I live."

With no warning whatsoever, Ellen pulled her car over into the nearest parking lot and turned off the engine. She stared at Matt in silence until he was so unnerved that he had to say something.

"What are you doing?" he managed to squeak out.

"How old are you?"

"I'm old enough!" Of course, saying that just proved the opposite.

"You said earlier, you said, 'when I get my license'," Ellen pushed.

"So?"

Ellen narrowed her eyes. "Means you're not Mully's age."

"I never said I was," Matt tried for a defiant tone, but only managed to sound younger.

"Who is Laddie?" Ellen asked in a dangerous tone.

"It's my last name?"

"You said you were Laddie's brother," she prompted.

"I am."

Matt shrunk into his seat as Ellen leaned forward and asked again, "Who is Laddie?"

"Fine! Shannon Laddie is my sister and she's a sophomore, well, about to be a junior and I'm going to be a freshman in just a couple weeks so I'm basically a high schooler now anyway."

"You haven't even started high school yet?" Ellen asked

with a sigh, tightening her hands on her steering wheel.

"Technically?" he whispered.

"Get out," Ellen said.

"No! What? No!" Matt instinctively grabbed the sides of his seat as if he would have to be dragged from the car.

"Come on, out," Ellen said as she undid her seatbelt.

She got out of the car. Glancing through the windshield, she saw Matt hesitate before undoing his seatbelt. He opened his door, got out and stood up. But the cold night air seemed to shock him back into his normal self.

He started babbling again as he approached her in front of the car. "Come on Ellen, I'm not that bad. We've been having fun, haven't we? We don't have to go anywhere. No one ever needs to see me. I'll deny I ever even met you. I live over on Maple Court. We can go straight there. Just please don't leave me here."

They were face-to-face in front of the car.

Ellen interrupted this passionate speech. "When's your birthday?"

"Next week," Matt answered, a grimace flickering across his face.

"So you're..."

"Thirteen." He was looking down at his shoes but couldn't help peeking at her. Ellen fought hard to keep her face neutral, and after a long moment of silence, he asked, "Why?"

She didn't answer.

"Why?" he persisted.

Ellen took a deep breath. "Tonight a thirteen-year-old I've never seen before bluffed his way into my car and managed to stay there for three hours."

"Are you going to call the cops?" Matt asked, his head

drooping in defeat.

"What? No! No, I..." Ellen smiled. "I have a feeling about you Matt Laddie. I think maybe you are going to be very cool someday."

Without elaborating, Ellen walked past him. Matt stood frozen in the headlights.

"Well?" Ellen called to his stunned back. "Do you want to learn how to drive stick or not?" She climbed into the passenger seat.

"Me?" Matt asked, turning slowly toward her as if he'd heard her from a great distance instead of four feet away.

"Get in before I change my mind," Ellen called out the window.

Matt almost tripped over his own feet turning around again and getting in on the driver's side. He had to move the seat forward and Ellen saw a blush creep across his face as he awkwardly bucked the seat to find the right distance to the pedals for his feet.

"I can do this, I can do this," he muttered under his breath.

Ellen looked away, biting her lip as she stared out the window at the otherwise deserted parking lot. There was plenty of room. There was nothing to hit. "This is crazy. He'll be fine. This is crazy," she muttered under her breath.

She turned back to him and began. "Ok Matt Laddie, first thing you're going to want to do is put your feet on the brake and the clutch pedals. No, left foot on the clutch and right on... that's the gas. Don't press that. Ok, so brake and clutch," she said with audible relief. He made a face and she continued before he could say anything, "Yes, at the same time! There you go. Ok, so next..."

20. Tonight, Tonight

Mully lay on the hood of her car, staring up at the stars. They were parked in their elementary school's parking lot but facing away from the streetlights so that the night sky was still visible. Music was playing just loudly enough to reach them through the car's open windows. Out of her left peripheral vision, she could see Trin pacing while she listened to a voicemail on her cell phone. On her right, AJ was sitting on the hood with his legs crossed. Ana leaned against the car next to him. Most people would have been amazed at how easily these two had fallen back into hanging out with each other, but Mully was surprised to find herself sad that Ana wasn't laying down with her head in AJ's lap. She used to find it annoying—or at least, weirdly intimate—that they were so comfortable being affectionate with each other around other people. But now she felt the wave of sadness again, because how many times had they ended up in those same positions, on this same car, listening to the same band as the minutes ticked through the middle of the night? *And now*, Mully thought with a sigh, *it's all going to be different.*

"Did you know you can pay to get a star named after someone?" AJ asked, interrupting her train of thought.

"Really?" Mully said, relieved to think about anything else.

"It's really expensive," Ana clarified.

"Oh yeah? Ready?" AJ countered.

"For what?" Ana asked, blinking in confusion.

"There." He pointed up at a random star in the sky. "I just named it."

A slight smile spread across Ana's face, until AJ said, "Behold the Carr Star." He cracked up laughing at his own joke. "And it didn't cost me a dime," he concluded smugly, looking back and forth between the two girls.

Mully didn't say anything, but she did look a little more fondly at the star. Ana got up and walked over to Trin. Her abrupt departure stopped AJ's laugh cold and he cleared his throat harder than strictly necessary before tipping his head back to stare at the sky again.

"Oh my god, AJ," Mully said after a moment.

"What?"

"*What?*" she repeated in shock. "What are you doing naming a star after me instead of Ana?"

"Carr Star sounds funny," AJ said defensively.

"I know but..." Mully trailed off and then shrugged, no idea how to explain.

A silence fell between them, and even though it wasn't awkward, Mully still felt like it was wrong. Usually, she and AJ never shut up around each other. They were always working on a script, or making a movie, or prepping a play, or arguing over what movie was Coppola's best. She had never felt tongue-tied like this around AJ before.

Mully frowned. That wasn't true. Freshman year, at the musical's wrap party at Mike T's house, Mully had had her first kiss. Aaron Cooper, a junior and one of the very few boys in the play, had been playing air hockey with her against AJ and Ana in the basement. When they won, he'd grabbed Mully in a big hug and kissed her. Mully had almost died of embarrassment, with AJ right there, who knew it was her first kiss. She cringed as she once again remembered how she had felt kind of mad too, because at that point, no one had expected Ana and AJ to last very long, and Mully had kind of, sort of, maybe, a little bit expected that when they broke up, she and AJ would get together and he would be her first kiss. So she'd done the only logical thing: she had avoided Aaron for the rest of the school year and never spoken about it again. Mully didn't know exactly what happened, but on the last day of school, AJ had approached her on Aaron's behalf to ask if she was okay and mad at him about something. *That* was the last time she hadn't known what to say around AJ.

Even now, all this time later, she could feel her face flushing and was grateful for the darkness as they looked up at the stars and listened to the music.

Trin closed up her phone and shoved it back into her messenger bag. She saw Ana walking toward her, head down, hands shoved into the pocket of her hoodie, and worried about what had happened while she was checking in with her mother.

"All good?" Ana asked.

"Yeah, we must have had a bad signal when she called, but she's fine now."

"We should probably start heading home anyway," Ana offered.

Trin shook her head no even as she said, "Sure. Eventually."

They started walking back over to the car.

"So do you have to get up early tomorrow? Or, I mean, later?" Trin asked as they walked across the parking lot.

"Not particularly. Check-in doesn't start until 11, and even with how slow my dad drives, it takes at most two hours."

"You nervous?" Trin asked quickly, before they got near AJ and Mully.

"I was, but," Ana glanced to make sure the others couldn't hear them. "I'm actually less nervous now that I know it's just me. That makes no sense, I know. But it's just like this whole added complication is no longer part of the day."

"So you guys really are broken up."

Ana hesitated before answering. "Yeah, I think so. But we'll still be friends, I guess."

Trin grinned at her. "You're, like, stupid brave, you know that?"   "Aw, shut up," Ana laughed.

Trin took in Mully and AJ on the hood of the Jag, staring up at the night sky as if everything weren't about to change in their lives. Ana was moving on. Maybe it was time for the rest of them to move on as well. Trin took a deep breath and quickly closed the last few steps over to her friends.

"So I've been thinking..." she said without preamble, as if continuing a conversation. Mully sat up, mirroring AJ's posture.

"About what?" AJ asked, still half staring up at the stars.

"About you!" Trin said as bluntly as she'd said anything in her entire life. She would force AJ to see reason, even if it was kind of terrifying to be yelling at her friend.

"Huh?" His head snapped down to look closer at her.

"Willer," Trin said as if it were obvious.

And it must have been obvious to AJ, because his response was, "Oh come on!"

Ana and Mully watched the exchange, transfixed by this strange turn of events.

AJ started to protest, but Trin talked over him, possibly for the first time in their friendship.

"No, listen," she said. "It's not NYU. It's not film school. But it IS college. You do two years there and transfer. You live at home and save up money—"

"I've already tried this," Mully said.

"Shut up," AJ blurted, and it wasn't clear if he meant

Mully or Trin or both of them.

"I'm serious!" Trin continued anyway. "We can't let graduating split us apart. And this will—"

"It wouldn't matter," AJ interrupted. "I'm not 'splitting us apart', Trin. I mean, whatever I do, Mully's leaving."

Mully cringed, and Trin jumped in to defend her. "She's going to school out west," Trin allowed.

"—But it's not like I'll never be back," Mully finished for her, and Trin nodded.

"You're leaving us behind," AJ said.

Trin saw Mully swallow hard and wished she would say something. Instead, Trin heard Ana finally come up behind her and start to say, "But AJ—"

"But AJ *what?*" AJ jumped off the hood of the car as he yelled at her. Both Mully and Trin instinctively leaned backwards away from him, but Ana stood her ground as AJ advanced on her. He towered threateningly over her, only inches away, and Trin would have felt the need to intervene if she hadn't caught sight of tears in his eyes.

"You're leaving us behind, too!" AJ yelled at Ana. "You think you're going to come home from New York City? You'll go to NYU and we'll be lucky if you stoop to hanging out with us during winter break because you'll be busy with all your new, big city friends instead of us. You *and* Mully'll both have other people that matter more and it will happen before you even realize it—but I'll realize it! You can count on that!"

Ana folded her arms across her chest, not backing down. "YOU don't get to be mad at ME Adam," she said evenly. "I thought you were going to be right there with me. That was the plan. That was what we've been talking about all summer."

Suddenly Trin felt hot tears burning in her own eyes. She just wanted them to stop. Stop yelling, stop saying they wouldn't hang out together. So even though she wasn't sure she'd be able to speak, she choked out, "You're all... leaving... and me? You're all so caught up... in your own drama that you don't even..." Trin took a deep breath that kept the tears from spilling over, but only just. "What am I supposed to do?" she asked quietly, looking at her friends' shoes instead of their eyes.

In a flash Mully was off the car and standing next to Trin, saying, "I thought you were excited for Willer!"

"I am! I'm..." Trin looked up at Mully's face—really looked at it. Stoic Mully, whose eyes were now glittering with tears. "I'm sorry," Trin said quickly. "I'm sorry, ok? I don't mean to be mad but I am. I just am."

"Are you... crying?" AJ asked Mully in shock.

"No!" Mully said, and of course her denial made the tears spill over and show her for the liar she was. Trin could feel the frustration radiating off Mully as she stomped a few feet back and turned away from them.

"I've known I was leaving for months but I didn't realize my friends hated me for it," Mully said as the tears kept rolling down her cheeks.

"We don't hate you," AJ said, looking horrified.

"Yeah, hate is a strong word," Ana agreed, nodding vigorously.

Trin shot Ana a look and said firmly to Mully, "We don't hate you."

"If everyone thinks we'll, like, never see each other again then, I... don't want to go," Mully said, crossing her arms over her chest as if hugging herself.

There was a moment of silence as the four of them

each took a breath and pulled themselves together.

"Yes, you do," Ana pointed out.

"Then I don't *want* to want to go," Mully said, glancing around as if hoping for someone to stop her from feeling this way.

"Come on," Trin said, suddenly looping her arm through Mully's and steering her away from the car.

"What?" Mully asked, using her other arm to wipe her face.

"We're going to take a walk," Trin insisted. She wasn't used to bossing Mully or AJ around, but she was finding that she was kind of good at it.

"Fine," Mully said in a strangled voice. She allowed Trin to lead her down the sidewalk in front of the school and out to the street.

"We don't hate you," Trin said again as they walked. "We love you and we'll miss you, ok?" She stopped under a streetlight and dug a pack of tissues out of her bag. "Stop using your cuff to wipe your nose, it's disgusting." She ripped out a few tissues and handed them to Mully.

Mully wiped her face properly and blew her nose. A couple cars full of kids drove past the school. Mully turned away from the road. Trin's hair made it impossible not to be seen, though, so she waved half-heartedly when Joe and Jerry honked hello.

"Ok, they're gone," Trin said.

"You think Ellen will miss me?" Mully asked.

Stunned by the out-of-nowhere question, it took Trin a moment to answer. "Of course! You're her only sister!"

"We're not like that though. She does her thing, I do mine..." Mully took a deep breath, ragged from all the crying, and muttered, "I didn't think going to California would be a big deal."

"Uh, of course it's a big deal!" Trin said, but she was quick to add, "But it will be ok. Of course it will be ok. It's always ok when people love each other."

Mully grinned at her cheesiness.

"Trin—" She cut herself off by suddenly hugging the stuffing out of Trin.

Trin knew Mully could only handle feelings for so long, so she pulled out of the embrace and briskly told her, "Just don't forget to thank us in your speeches when you win a million awards."

"I promise," Mully said with one last sniffle.

Matt glanced at Ellen out of the corner of his eye. "How am I doing?" he asked. She could hear the hope in his voice.

"You could certainly be worse," Ellen allowed.

"Really?" His grin practically lit up the car's interior.

"That's not the compliment you seem to think it is."

But she smiled back at him to soften the blow. Matt wasn't even bad at driving, especially considering it was a stick... Ellen just wasn't sure her stomach would ever fully recover from this evening. She wondered how her parents had survived teaching her and Mully to drive. Maybe when it was your own kid it wasn't so bad.

Matt had already worked his way up to driving on the Post Road, with all the starting and stopping at lights that it required. Each one made Ellen grip her door handle a little harder, but he was doing it, and when he hit a lucky streak of green lights, she could almost relax and just be a normal passenger.

"This guy is running up on us," Matt said, flicking his gaze between the road and the rear view mirror.

Ellen turned around and immediately turned back towards the front, the color drained from her face. "Oh for God's—" She seemed to remember that Matt was in the car with her. "Just stay in this lane. Just keep going," she told him.

Ellen closed her eyes, almost as if she were saying a prayer in her head, and only opened them when she heard the change in the air through Matt's open window. If she were going to have to talk to Jack, she certainly wasn't going to let him see that she'd been dreading it.

"Well, this is a change. The passenger seat?" Jack Cadwallyn called over to them.

"What do you want, Jack?" Ellen yelled past Matt.

"Who the hell are you?" Jack asked Matt, ignoring her.

"I'm Matt—"

"What do you WANT, Jack?" Ellen cut Matt off.

"So hostile, jeez!" Jack clutched his right hand to his heart in mock pain. "I'm just saying hi."

"Hi," Ellen deadpanned.

"You gonna be around tonight?"

"Highly unlikely," she answered.

"What are you, chicken?" Jack asked with a smile.

"Go to hell, Jack."

He kept smiling despite her iciness and addressed Matt instead. "What about you, little man? You feel up to a race?"

"Dude, you're driving a station wagon," Matt said.

There was a beat where Ellen saw the rage flit across Jack's face. She doubted Matt would have recognized it, but he seemed to notice that he touched a nerve as he tightened his hands on the steering wheel.

But all Jack did was give them the finger and peel off. When his car was just a set of red taillights, Ellen let out a huge sigh and started to laugh.

"That was brilliant," she told Matt.

"I was just being honest," he said, wrinkling his forehead.

"Take a right up here," Ellen directed him.

"Towards...?"

"Nowhere in particular. Just keep driving."

Ellen settled back in the passenger seat. She didn't hold the door handle anymore, just allowed herself a slight wince as she felt the car struggle under Matt's guidance. Then it righted itself and she turned up the music.

23. So I Fall Again

AJ collapsed against the hood of Mully's car. He half-sat, one foot on the ground and one propped up on the bumper, and stared at the pavement. Ana stood a few feet away, not saying anything. It was not a comfortable silence. Mully had left her keys on the car's hood and AJ grabbed them, desperate to DO anything. He threw the keys up in the air and caught them one-handed over and over. The noise they made provided some relief from his ex-girlfriend staring at him.

Ana uncrossed her arms. "So what do you think of Trin's Willer idea?" she finally asked so quietly he almost didn't hear her.

AJ kept his eyes on the keys and shrugged.

"Didn't you make any plans?" she tried. "You said you've known since graduation."

Silence. Keys in the air. Jangling together. Hit the apex, then down until they landed with a thump in AJ's hand. Toss them skyward again.

"You had the whole summer..."

"Don't start," was all AJ said.

"I'm not starting!" Ana said, finally losing her temper. "I'm giving you the benefit of the doubt. If you've had two months to think about it—I just know you and I know how you make plans. You have to have a plan."

He stopped tossing the keys. AJ stared at her: this beautiful, smart, funny, talented woman who had not only tolerated but full-on liked him. Ana had always been out of his league and yet, it had always just seemed to work between them. He didn't realize they *knew* each other so well. Because of course she was right: he loved making plans. He loved strategizing and playing things out in his head ahead of time. He rarely took chances, and even then, only when he figured he had a good chance at succeeding. Which was why this whole summer had been so infuriating to him. Because now he had to admit the truth.

"I don't. I've got no plans and no ideas. I've got nothing." AJ stopped playing with the keys and just stared at them in his hands.

"That's disappointing," Ana said.

"You're disappointed in me," he muttered. It wasn't a question.

"Yup," she answered anyway.

He jerked his head up but didn't say anything.

"What? What did you expect me to say?" Ana asked him.

AJ didn't have an answer for her. He didn't have a plan for himself. This summer had been the first time in his life AJ had felt so lost, and he had dealt with it by pretending it wasn't happening. Now, tonight, it was happening. He was surprised by how angry he was. He had always had a sarcastic edge, and Jack knew how to push his buttons, but this rage at the world was something new.

"Let's go," he said, looking at the keys instead of Ana. "I hate it here." He looked up at her and the parking lot with its lights and the strip of grass and sidewalk, and he knew he meant it.

She was staring at him like he was crazy.

"I hate it here," he said again. "I feel like we've spent

our whole lives in these parking lots."

"We can't leave Trin and Mully," Ana pointed out, glancing at the two silhouettes over by the road.

"It's a short walk to the diner," he said, singling out Mully's car key on the key ring.

"Don't be a jerk AJ." Ana's brow furrowed in annoyance. "You're better than that," she added.

"Am I?" he asked, honestly curious. He didn't feel better than that right now. He felt exactly like the type of person who could drive to the diner with a beautiful girl and make his friends walk over later.

"Yes!" Ana's explosive response cut into his worried brain. She was closer to him now. Maybe things could go back to the way they had been. He had never had these sorts of thoughts when they were together. Maybe Ana was the key to fixing him.

AJ took a shaky breath and practically whispered. "How do you know?" he asked her.

"Because I know you," Ana said, exasperated. "You're better than that. You just are. You're not that guy. I know because... I still trust you even if I don't love you anymore."

It was like a black cloud rolled in front of his field of vision. The vulnerability AJ had been allowing to show went back under the mask of anger on his face as he shoved it down.

"Please consider what Trin said," Ana said, her words suddenly uneasy. Then, after a moment, she added, "I still care about you."

AJ pushed up off the car and past her, saying "Let's go find them and get out of here."

"Ok."

He was already several parking spots away when he heard her sandals slapping against the pavement as she caught up to him. AJ didn't let himself turn around.

24. Crash into Me

Ellen hummed along to the radio. Once, this had been her and Jack's song. For a long time, she hadn't been able to stand to listen to it, but now... now it wasn't so bad. She could just hang out in her car, her right arm dangling out the window, a little cold but not so cold that she had to pull it back in. It had been a long time since she was a passenger. Even though she was the better driver and had the cooler car, Ellen had always let Jack drive because, well, because he was the boy. Boys drove their girlfriends. Boys also decided when you were ready to have sex and who your friends should be and how much beer you could handle... Ellen smirked. That was one of the most important lessons she had ever learned: all of that was sexist bullshit, and you didn't have to go along with any of it.

She looked over at Matt driving. The breeze was ruffling his hair, and his eyes were locked on the road in front of them, concentrating. Ellen felt her shoulders tensing up in an old fight-or-flight response to being in the passenger seat while someone else was in control of the car. She made herself relax. She hoped she hadn't set him up to be an asshole by teaching him to drive. Matt was a good kid. Hopefully he would turn into a good guy. She made herself look back out the window. They were close to the river and she was on the verge of suggesting they swing by when she looked at the clock.

"Hey, we absolutely don't have to, but do you want to

go home?" she asked Matt.

He started to say no, but he looked at the clock and practically stalled the car. It was almost 2:00 am.

"Can I drive there?" Matt asked.

"Yes," Ellen assured him.

"Then... ok."

They fell back into companionable silence as he made his way across town.

As they got closer to his neighborhood, Matt kept shifting in his seat, obviously itching to say something. "I just want to say... thank you," he said finally.

"For teaching you to drive," Ellen said, looking out the window and remembering all of her late summer nights as she watched the night-dark trees flit past.

"For letting me in the car," Matt said.

She whipped her head around, surprised. "You got yourself in the car," Ellen told him. She laughed, not at him. "It's not like I had anything better to do tonight," she added.

"I guess driving around with me isn't what you wanted to do though," he said.

"It was fine. I used to do this with Mully all the time." *When did that stop?* she continued to herself.

Matt nodded. "It must be weird knowing she's leaving."

"How did you even know about all that anyway? About my sister and her friends?" It was the one piece of the puzzle Ellen still couldn't figure out.

"My sister did drama and talks about them all the time," Matt confessed. "Plus, Mully is probably the first person in the history of Norford High to go to college in California. She literally makes movies. And you were with Jack when he crashed racing on Miskwa Hill. Your family is, like, basically famous."

Ellen frowned. "That's nothing to be famous about."

"Look at this car!" Matt protested.

Ellen turned her frown to the window and muttered, "At least Mully is famous for something she's doing herself."

"Are you going to miss her?"

"She's my baby sister," Ellen said by way of answering.

Matt shook his head. "If I went across the country, my sister wouldn't miss me."

"Yes she would," Ellen said.

Matt came around the last curve before his house, the only house on this section of the road. The two-story home was tucked up on a small hill, and surrounded by trees on three sides. A light was on over the front door. "Well, here we are—"

As the headlights swept across his front yard, they illuminated a giant buck towering over them.

"Stop," Ellen nearly screamed.

"But—"

"Just stop. Now!" she hissed.

The car jerked to a stop. They stared up at the deer. Yes, he was on a hill but even without that advantage, he was obviously enormous. Matt and Ellen looked at him. He looked at them. The deer flicked one of its ears.

"Put it in reverse," Ellen whispered, her heart hammering. The thing was huge. Bigger than any deer she had seen in her entire life. If it rammed the car—the car would lose. He would open it up like a tin can with those antlers. "Just pull out of the driveway very slowly."

Matt went for the gear shift, and pressed a pedal. With a grind and a halt, the car stalled.

"Careful..." Ellen didn't dare take her eyes off the stag.

She had thought antlers like that were only in cartoons. Matt tried again, and managed to get the car rolling backwards inch by painful inch. Ellen moved her lips in a silent prayer as they reached the end of the driveway and turned onto the road.

"Not too fast." She was still whispering as they began to drive back down his street.

"Ok," Matt whispered back.

She waited until they were around the curve and out of sight of Matt's house before she said, "I think we should drive around some more."

"That's..." Matt was having trouble breathing normally. "That's absolutely ok with me."

25. Sugar High

As Ana got closer to Trin and Mully, she could hear them singing "Detachable Penis" as they walked down the sidewalk with arms linked, and her heart ached a little. She had just wanted to spend the evening like that: being silly with her friends. Instead, she'd ended up in a shouting match with AJ. She tried to look over at him without being caught in his eye line. She worried that she had done absolutely nothing to make things any better, and now he might not even consider Trin's advice.

Trin called out, "Hey! What's next?"

"You ready to get out of here?" AJ asked them.

Both girls said, "Sure," Trin loudly and confidently, Mully muttering it at the sidewalk. But Ana could barely hear either of them as their words were drowned out by a car that drove past, stopped, then reversed to where Trin and Mully stood. Ana and AJ ran over to join them, recognizing the station wagon.

Jack rolled down the passenger-side window to talk, ignoring the fact that he was stopped in the middle of the street.

"Well, well, well, if it isn't Adam and his girlfriends," he said with a giant grin.

"What do you want, Jack?" AJ demanded.

"Just saying hi," Jack said, waving his hand innocently.

"Hi," Mully said, her voice dripping with sarcasm.

Jack smirked at her and turned his attention to Ana instead. She started as he asked her, "You guys done driving around?"

"I suppose. Might head home soon," Ana managed to answer. She had never been able to entirely relax around Jack.

"But the night is young!" Jack said.

"It's almost—" AJ began.

"If you want," Jack interrupted, still speaking just to Ana, "we could drive around a little."

Ana knit her brows together, but for a moment she didn't say anything. It sounded almost like he was flirting with her—which was insane since he was her boyfriend's older brother. Or, ex-boyfriend, but still! However, it was almost like a cloud lifted where Jack was concerned. An older guy she wasn't interested in was hitting on her? Ana knew just what to do.

"Go the hell, Jack," Ana said lightly.

"Didn't you hear?" he responded, not a hint of reproach in his voice. "I was technically dead. So, I mean, probably, right?"

She saw AJ ball his hands into fists and Mully open her mouth to yell at Jack. Ana panicked for a moment, unsure who to move toward first. She didn't have enough time to decide before Jack spoke instead.

"Your sister walked away," he snarled at Mully. She shut her mouth. Ana took a deep breath of relief as AJ also backed down.

Ana took a step toward Jack's car and said clearly, "We're not interested." Then, without thinking, she stuck her tongue out at him.

"Fine," Jack said.

"See you at home," AJ yelled sarcastically at the car as

he pulled away. Jack half-heartedly waved his hand out his window.

"Should we..." Trin started.

"Yeah, let's get going," Mully said.

Ana was still looking at Jack's station wagon's taillights.

"I think I just want to go home," she said, her forehead scrunched up in thought. Why had she done that at the end? It was almost like *she* was flirting! She didn't even like Jack as a person! Why would she encourage him? She closed her eyes for a moment, shaking her head. Her brain hurt.

Mully started herding everyone back to her car, saying to Ana, "I'll drop you at the diner. I'm going to drive around some more."

AJ bit out, "Trying to be as cool as Jack?"

Mully glared at him in disgust. "No. It's just that, like, it's already late and it's my last night. It would be kind of cool to stay up and see the sunrise."

AJ laughed as he visibly softened and told her, "That is so cheesy."

Ana was annoyed with herself and with them and she didn't really understand why in either case. "I can't, my parents still have me on curfew," she said to interrupt their moment.

"I told you, I'll drop you off next," Mully said.

She was already mostly in the car when Trin said, "Can you believe we were ever little enough to go here?"

Everyone stopped and stared at Trin looking up at the school. It had seemed so huge and intimidating when they were students, and even once they moved on to middle school, it was still a gigantic brick building. Now, Ana could swear she could reach out and touch the roof.

Mully shivered and sat down in her driver's seat, pulling her door shut.

AJ half-smiled at Trin. "I have the cheesiest friends in the entire world," he said before getting into the car with Mully.

Ana looked over the top of the car at Trin. She had made AJ happy again, and Ana felt incredibly grateful. "Elementary, my dear Watson," she told Trin with a smile before they both got into the backseat.

Mully pulled out of the parking lot and cranked up the soundtrack to *Empire Records* as they drove off into the night.

26. Smooth

Matt held his breath as he approached his house and felt a smile grow as the headlights lit up an empty lawn and driveway. He eased the car up and put it in park before daring to look at Ellen.

"Well, we made it," she said, relief in her voice.

"No Bambi," he nodded, grinning at her.

"That was Bambi's dad," Ellen laughed.

"So... ok," Matt said. Slowly, reluctantly, he slid his hands off the steering wheel. He knew he would never drive a car as cool as this one again, and his head was full of conflicting thoughts. He was sad that the night was over, but the thrill of everything he'd done and seen was still rushing through him.

Matt was unsure what to say and both of them stayed silent as they opened their doors and got out of the car. There was an awkward moment when they had to do the back-and-forth dance to pass each other in front of the car, and Ellen let out another laugh.

Matt looked up at her face and knew from the tips of his hair to his toes that she was the most beautiful girl he would ever know. He suddenly, fiercely wished that she would kiss him, but she just dodged around him and climbed into the driver's seat, completely missing the look on his face.

Which is for the best, he thought, watching her. He didn't want her to remember him as some adoring little puppy. He committed her laugh to memory and convinced himself that it was enough that he had made her laugh like that. Not meanly, not mockingly, but a pure, joyful sound that exploded out of Ellen Carr and washed over him. Suddenly he knew he had to say something. Matt rushed over to Ellen's window.

Ellen was adjusting her seat and mirrors when Matt bent over and leaned into the car. He pushed aside the rush of awe that just minutes ago, he had been the one sitting in that driver's seat and instead, he forced his mouth to function so he could actually express how much this evening had meant to him.

"Thank you, Ellen Carr," he said seriously.

"See you around Matt Laddie." She smiled at him. It made him feel even warmer than a kiss.

He stood back from the car and watched her reverse out of the driveway and take off down his street. Matt sighed and looked up at the sky. There were a few stars and the moon and a warm breeze and he just wanted to lie down on his lawn and never go inside. But after a moment, he jogged up his front steps and let himself into the house as quietly as possible. If he didn't go inside, he would never get to see the look on his sister's face tomorrow when he told her who he'd been hanging out with tonight.

27. The Way Things Are

Ellen drove slowly through the twisty back roads of Matt's neighborhood. *Well, that was interesting,* she thought to herself. She glanced at the clock and grimaced. Not that she had to be home, but she was going to be *so* tired tomorrow morning. She could drive the roads to her house almost on autopilot and she let herself sink into the music on the radio instead of thinking about anything.

Her parents always left the garage door open for her, and Ellen was able to pull straight in to her parking spot. Both of her parents' cars were parked in front of the other half of the garage, and Mully would get stuck out on the driveway too, as usual.

Ellen got out of her car and stretched as tall as she could. She bent back over and grabbed her purse out of the car before closing the door and locking it up. Only then did she let herself look over at the other car in the garage. Mully had been so mad that the space was taken up by a car that didn't run, but they couldn't possibly leave this out.

Ellen walked over as if hypnotized and ran a hand lovingly along the fender of what had been a Dino 246 GTS. Built in Italy in 1971, it *technically* hadn't been road-legal in the United States, but it was so close to the Series III versions—which *were* legal—that hardly anyone could tell. She remembered her dad singing old Rat Pack songs while they worked on it in this very garage. She had been all excited because she thought they were getting a Ferrari brought over, and Ellen could laugh now at how as an angry 14-year-old, she had stamped her foot and yelled, "That's not a Ferrari!" Her dad had just looked up lovingly and told her, "No, it's even better. And it can be yours if we get it running." From that moment on, the Dino had been her pride and joy. Before its arrival, her dad's gas station and garage was respectable, but after she started driving the bright red sports car around, it became infamous. Everyone knew the Carrs after that. So of course, it was the car Jack had been driving when they crashed. Now it lay crumpled in her parents' garage.

Whenever Ellen thought about the Dino, her memories got all mixed up and layered on top of each other. Rubbing it so the red paint job shone. Red blood on Jack's face. Dad teaching her to dance to "Everybody Loves Somebody" next to the car. The radio still playing even after the crash so that one of the cops had to reach in and turn it off. The first time she ever shifted gears in it. Seeing it out the window as she rode in an ambulance for the first time. Her dad hanging up the kitchen phone so excited he was still speaking Italian as he started to tell her mom about the car being available. Her dad hanging up the kitchen phone to tell her that Jack was going to live. The exact shade between white and yellow of the chamois she used to dry the car. The exact shade between white and yellow of the cast on her left arm.

If she stared at the busted-up car any longer, she knew she was going to start crying. Ellen could feel it tugging at the corners of her mouth, wanting her to give in to being sad because she hadn't been able to bring herself to start working on fixing it. There were too many memories wrapped up in that metal.

She walked over to the string hanging from the

garage's light bulb and pulled it hard to turn off the light. Then she slapped the garage door button to close it and walked out, fully intending to go inside and throw herself onto her bed to sleep. It had been a long, weird night.

No! her mind screamed at her, and before she even knew what she was doing, Ellen ducked under the closing door back into the garage. She hit the door to send it back up again and yanked the string to turn the light on so her parents would know she was still out.

Ellen got into her car, turned up the radio, and roared off back out into the night.

28. Sleep Now in the Fire

Mully pulled her car into the diner parking lot and took the spot right next to Ana's car.

"I am so going to miss curfew," Ana admitted, looking at the time.

"So stay out," AJ said before he could think about it.

"If you're already in trouble, what's the harm?" Mully added.

Ana scoffed at them. "I'll be fine. But there's a big difference between being twenty minutes late and four hours late."

But no one got out of the car. The four friends just sat there looking at each other, not sure what to say now that the last moments together were finally here.

"All right," Ana said, psyching herself up to go. She couldn't look at AJ because she had no idea how to feel about him, but she knew she needed to say *something* before they all split up. When would she see AJ next? When would she see any of them? "All right, all right, all right. See you guys tomor—around." She laughed at her mistake. "Mully... Mully you are going to have the best time in California, ok?"

She leaned forward and hugged the driver's seat and Mully in it. Mully laughed and reached a hand up to give Ana's arm a squeeze in return.

"Bye—" Mully had to clear her throat. "Bye Ana. See you at Christmas."

Ana let go and opened her door.

"Buon Natale chica," she said with a smile. Then Ana let her gaze slide over to AJ, even though she hadn't meant to. He looked back at her with his blue eyes and it felt like a thunderbolt hit straight through her chest. With a gulp of air, Ana made herself stand up, close the door, and walk around the back of the car over to hers. Like a robot, she got her keys out of her bag and let herself in.

Her three friends watched in silence as Ana got into her car and drove away with a small wave. Mully blinked a few times but managed not to cry as she pictured Ana arriving in New York the next morning, alone, just like Mully would be when she got to California.

Trin started fishing for her keys in her messenger bag. "I'm pretty tired. Guess I should head home too."

"Come on," Mully protested. "Your parents never care how late you stay out anymore."

"I know but—"

"Sunrise or bust!" AJ said in mock excitement.

Trin smiled but she shook her head. "No way guys. I know it's your last night but I can't stay up an entire night."

"Trin..." Mully didn't know if she had words left for another goodbye. *How* had she not realized she would have to go through this tonight?

The two girls lunged across the center console and caught each other in a hug.

"It's going to be so weird without you," Mully said into Trin's blue hair.

"I'll go online every day," Trin assured her. They pulled apart enough to look each other in the eyes. "We can talk all the time."

"We will," Mully vowed. "Be good, Trin."

As Trin let herself out of the car, Mully tried to keep herself from tearing up—*again*. She felt a frown pull on her face and twitched her face muscles in an attempt to look calm.

"Ok," she whispered to AJ. She restarted her car and backed out of the parking spot.

They passed Trin at her car as they turned back toward the street. Trin was hastily wiping her eyes but she smiled up at them. Both AJ and Mully leaned out their windows.

"See you!" AJ yelled.

"Give 'em hell!" Mully said.

Trin's forehead wrinkled in confusion. "At Willer?"

Mully whipped her head around to shout back at her. "Everywhere!"

They pulled their heads back into the car. Mully put her blinker on and turned right onto the Post Road.

29. Try Again

Trin watched Mully and AJ drive off together, just like they always did. Trin felt herself smiling before she even realized she was doing it. They were best friends. They were *her* best friends, and it didn't matter that they were all splitting up.

She turned back to her driver's side door. Key in hand, she went to stick it in the lock, but before she could let herself in, a minivan pulled up and stopped right behind her. The side door was flung open and Trin spun around.

Before Trin could say anything or even process what was happening, two girls jumped out. One pulled a hoodie over her head backwards, the hood covering her face. Then it felt like someone was duct taping her arms to her sides; she froze, unable to even think. She just managed to shout, "Hey!" when they moved the duct tape roll up to secure the hood of the sweatshirt over her head.

They pulled her into the van, and it started moving.

Trin strained to see against the blackness of the sweatshirt hood taped up over her face. She could hear TLC on the radio, and laughter. Neither sound seemed right for having been snatched off the street. She smelled weed, which at least the D.A.R.E. program *had* warned her would be used by evil villains looking to steal her virginity. But it didn't sound like—

Someone pulled the duct tape off her head and let the hood drop so she could see. Trin blinked rapidly and looked around. She was sitting in the middle row of a minivan driven by a slightly older girl. Another girl the same age sat in the passenger seat, smoking a bowl of weed. Trin didn't recognize either of them, but then she turned and saw Megan sitting next to her. Sarah was sitting in the back row, looking terrified.

"Better?" Megan asked, yanking off the tape around her arms.

"What's going on?" Trin managed to ask.

The driver glanced back at them with a snort of laughter. "Sorry if we scared you. Most people know we're coming."

Sarah leaned forward to talk to Trin over the music. "My sister warned me there was an initiation, but I wasn't sure if I was allowed to say anything when we talked earlier. And she didn't mention we would literally be kidnapped." Sarah glared at the driver.

"Initiation?" Trin was still completely lost.

"Welcome to Willer!" crowed the girl in the passenger seat.

Trin stared at her, still drawing a blank.

"You're going to Willer?" the older girl prompted.

"Yes..."

"You've been selected for initiation," the driver said, as if that explained everything.

Trin spoke slowly. "But I'm not in a sorority or anything."

The passenger shrugged. "It's just that, like, kids from Norford High have been going to Willer for forever so there are, like, these things you have to do. Like, you know, rituals." She talked so fast that Trin worried she had misunderstood.

But she caught that last word all right.

"Rituals?"

"Sarah's sis said it's no big deal," Megan whispered.

"Yeah, but she also left out kidnapping," Trin whispered back.

"Just come with us," the passenger said, as if they had a choice. She half-turned in her seat and reached out to shake hands with them. "I'm Nikki by the way. That's Jessica," she pointed at the driver, "and we'll be your happy hosts this evening." She giggled.

Trin shook her hand, still dazed. She was saved from having to say anything by the song on the radio changing to a new one she didn't recognize. But she was obviously the only person in the car who didn't.

"Yes!" Nikki shrieked, turning up the volume. Trin could even hear Sarah singing along behind her. Trin bobbed her head nervously in time with the music. It was good; she just felt like an idiot for not knowing it. Hadn't it played at prom a few months ago?

She was distracted from her own thoughts when a cell phone in the center console rang. Nikki turned down the music and answered it one-handed, all without putting down her pipe. The three girls in the backseat listened intently to her side of the conversation, hoping for clues about these so-called rituals.

"Hello? Hey. But you're supposed to be getting the guys. We've got our three. Really? But we—Fine. No, no, it's fine. K, bye."

She snapped the phone shut and tossed it back into a cup holder.

"We have to go get Will Thomas," she told Jessica.

"He's taller than we are!" Jessica protested. "How are we supposed to do that?"

Nikki shrugged. "I'm sure it will be fine. But they went to his house and he wasn't there, and now Mike says he's going to be late if they have to loop back around town to find him."

It was like someone else had control of Trin's body because she heard herself volunteering the information, "He was at the high school earlier."

"No, they stopped playing when Derek went to the diner," Megan said. "But they were going to walk down to the Millers'. They've got to still be in that area."

"You guys are the best," Jessica said as she banged a U-ey to go back down the Post Road in the right direction. Another song that Trin didn't recognize came on the radio and she felt herself blushing, glad no one could see her in the darkness of the van. She was also horribly aware of being the only person wearing Converse sneakers in this vehicle. And of how outrageously blue her hair was. Trin wished she could melt right into her seat and disappear.

Nikki handed Jessica the bowl, and without missing a beat, she leaned forward to steer with her forearms while taking a hit. Even though Trin didn't do drugs, it was impossible not to be impressed at the coordination.

"Anyone else?" Jessica said in a cloud of smoke when she was done. Nikki took back the bowl and lighter and held them out to the back seats.

Megan took a drag, but Trin and Sarah shook their heads no. Nikki took it back from Megan and turned around, still happy as a clam. No judgment. Take a hit, don't take a hit, either was fine with these girls. Trin felt herself relax the teeniest bit.

Jessica tore past the high school and down the side streets near Flicker Street.

"Stop!" Nikki finally shouted.

The car screeched to a halt and Jessica reversed to look down a cul-de-sac. A group of boys were at the dead end, setting off fountain fireworks.

"That him?" Jessica asked, putting the car in park and squinting down the road.

"Yeah," Nikki said, already taking off her seatbelt. "Megan, want to help again?"

"Anyone else want a turn?" Megan asked the other two girls.

"I-I'll go," Trin said before she could change her mind, a thrill running through her.

Nikki grabbed another black Willer hoodie from the pile between her feet and tossed Trin the roll of duct tape.

"Pull some," Megan suggested.

"Huh?"

"The duct tape," she pointed at the roll. "Start ripping it now so you don't get stuck. That's what happened to me the first time and it was totally embarrassing."

"Thanks," Trin said, awkwardly tearing at the roll of tape. Luckily, four years of drama club had made her a duct tape expert. But she was pretty sure it was the first time Megan had ever admitted to not being perfect at something.

As if on cue, the radio started playing "Insane in the Brain".

I must be insane, Trin thought.

"Ready?" Nikki asked, her hand on the side door handle.

Trin took a deep breath and put her hand on the sliding door's handle. "Yep."

They nodded at each other. Jessica put the car in drive and turned onto the road, driving way too fast for the short distance. Just as she wrenched the car sideways and stopped,

Nikki and Trin jumped out.

Trin almost tripped, but found her feet as Nikki rounded the other side of the van, hoodie in hand. A crazed grin on her face, Nikki hopped up to get enough height to get the hoodie over Will, and Trin advanced with the tape ready.

Will's friends seemed surprised, but started both cheering and mocking him as the girls spun Will around and herded him into the van. She and Nikki sort of threw him onto the minivan's floor before jumping in themselves. Trin slid into the middle row right after him and rolled the door closed. Jessica floored it back up the road away from the fireworks. Trin could hear the guys still laughing and yelling even over the blaring music inside the van.

Megan had climbed into the backseat with Sarah to make room in the middle row for Trin and Will, who was still on the floor. Trin put her arms under Will's armpits and tried to lift him up onto the seat properly.

"Uh, you guys aren't who I was expecting," Will yelled through his hood, "so if this isn't—"

Trin ripped the duct tape off to pull down his hood. Even though his arms were still pinned to his sides and his hair looked completely crazy, his face transformed into a smile as he recognized her.

"Hi you," he said, grinning.

"Uh, hi," Trin grunted as she tried to lift him again. Now that he was using his legs to cooperate, she was able to help him onto the seat, which gave her enough room to unwrap his arms.

He started to thank her but everyone's attention was stolen by Nikki saying, "Ok, that's Megan, Sarah, Katrina, and Will. We are good to roll!"

"Who's Katrina?" Will asked, looking around. "Oh,

Trin. Whoa, I never thought about that before."

"It's actually short for Trinity. Like in *The Matrix*?"

"I love that movie," he told her.

"So you prefer Trin?" Jessica asked over her shoulder as she drove them to wherever these "rituals" would take place.

Trin shrugged. "It's just a nickname. I don't care what people call me."

"What kind of bullshit is that?" Nikki said, turning around. "You have to care what people call you."

"Trin's a good name," Megan said. "Katrina sounds too stuffy for you."

Trin practically jumped in her seat. Megan Taylor had an opinion on her name? And it almost sounded like she *liked* Trin.

"What other nicknames are there for Katrina?" Will asked.

"Duh, Kat?" Nikki suggested.

Jessica meowed.

"No, K-A-T," Nikki said, sounding annoyed.

"I kind of like that," Trin started to say, "But I don't know..." She should have melted into her seat when she had the chance. It turned out being the center of attention was actually worse than being invisible. She could feel everyone except Jessica looking at her and she felt a blush burning across her face. She was so glad no one could see it in the dark interior of the minivan.

"Come on, we start college next week," Will said in a kind voice. "You can be whatever you want." Noticing the blush in the passing-by headlights of another car, he changed the tone of the conversation. "Hey, maybe I'll start going by Billy."

"*Billy Thomas?*" Megan exploded with laughter.

"Hi Billy, I'm Kat," Trin said, immediately picking up on the joke he'd made to help deflect attention from her. "Well, that sounds insane," she said, clearly saying *thank you* with her eyes.

"I've heard worse," Jessica said as she put on her blinker and took a left.

"Hi Kat, I'm... Bill?" Will tried instead.

And just like that, everyone was coming up with variations on their names.

"Pleased to meet you Meggy, my name is William," Will said in his most formal tone.

"Oh, do call me Nicole," Nikki said, almost hysterical.

"Sarah doesn't have any nicknames," Sarah whined.

"Oh shut up Sissy," Megan teased her.

"Why Jessie, I'd recognize you anywhere!" Will said, but Jessica snapped them out of it.

"Hey everyone, shut up. We're here," she announced.

30. Walking After You

Mully's Jag inched through the parking lot of the All Saints Elementary School as she looked for a good place to park. Mully wanted a break from driving, to just sit and listen to music for a while. But there were a surprising amount of cars around, all with steamed-up windows.

"Ok, really?" she said in disgust as she pulled back out onto the street and kept driving.

"What?" AJ asked.

"How can people make out there? Jesus is literally staring down at them!"

"You don't notice," AJ said offhand.

"Oh my god... you've! You!" Mully was shocked but laughing. It really wasn't a surprise when she thought about how long he and Ana had been dating.

"Well, uh," AJ shifted uncomfortably in his seat. He hung his arm out the window and laughed at his own embarrassment. "So keep driving," he finally said. "Go to the middle school instead."

"No, people will definitely be making out there," Mully dismissed it out of hand.

"Oh, are we speaking from experience?" He smiled at her.

"Shut up AJ." She stared straight ahead at the road.

"Maybe we should go the middle school," he mused.

She didn't respond.

The middle school was coming up on their left and he couldn't resist narrating, "And... we're just driving right past it... Cool, that's cool."

She smirked, still not saying anything.

They kept driving. Without telling AJ her plan, Mully turned into the high school parking lot. She drove around back so that no one would see her car from the road and recognize it. It wasn't until they got out and were locking their doors that she realized there were people having sex in another two cars parked in back. She and AJ shot each other a look and had a whole conversation in a moment of eye contact. They both closed up the car and walked quickly past the other vehicles to the stairs down to the football field.

"So we're back here," AJ said as they bounced down the steps. "I can't believe it."

"What's the big deal? We have to kill at least another hour somewhere," Mully said.

"Hour?"

"Isn't that when sunrise is?" Mully almost tripped in the dark.

"I guess," AJ said, shooting out an arm to steady her.

"You just don't want to go home," she pointed out.

"Maybe I like spending time with you," he scoffed.

"Since when?" Mully asked.

"Uh, since 1989? When you had a Star Wars birthday party and became my best friend?"

"Whatever, nerd." She smiled. It was lighter enough by the football field that he could see her face, and he smiled in return.

They walked past the football field and climbed over the short fence that separated the baseball diamond from the other playing fields.

Mully started running and flapping her arms. "Look, I'm an angel in the outfield!"

"I know I'm no sports expert, but I'm pretty sure that's not how baseball works."

"Party pooper," Mully called back at him, but she stopped running and let him catch up to her before continuing, "The only thing I know about baseball is the sex equivalent bases thing. And even that I learned from *Wonder Years.*"

"Like, Winnie Cooper *Wonder Years*?" AJ said quickly.

"Yeah. They're walking around a baseball field and talking about it and then they kiss."

"No they don't! They go on the swings after that. They kiss in the pilot when they're sitting on the big rock," AJ insisted.

"Since when do you know *The Wonder Years* so well?" she asked.

AJ looked up at the starry sky and said wistfully, "You don't forget Winnie Cooper."

"You are such a boy," Mully teased, turning so that he would bump into her hard with his next step.

"Well, yeah, usually," AJ said as he caught his balance.

"Guess so." Mully was ahead of him again.

"Mully, stop," he said, standing stock still.

Something about the way he said her name made Mully stop in her tracks. She turned around and felt the air sucked out of her body. The way he was looking at her—he had never run his eyes over her like that before. Sometimes she *wished* he would look at her like that, but now that it had happened it was overwhelming. Mully stared down at the grass as she shuffled over to him, somewhat unsure that it had really happened.

"What's up?" she said without looking up.

AJ put his hands on her shoulders to get her to look up at him. To her dismay, her heart started pounding.

"Do you want me to kiss you?" he asked.

"What?" she bluffed.

"Look at us. Look at us walking around here. And you bring up the bases..."

Mully shrugged out from under his arms. "Let's keep walking."

He started walking again, and now he was the one looking at his feet. Mully jumped over a base sticking up from the dirt. A smile flickered across AJ's face as he got an idea. AJ stomped his foot down when he reached it and announced, "Second base."

"Cut it out," Mully snapped before she could stop herself. Her heart was still wrenching inside her chest.

"Too late. I know you too well. Little Miss Completionist. If you don't go step on third too, it will drive you insane." AJ was grinning and it made her relax too. Plus, he was right, and she knew it would totally bug her if she didn't beat him to third.

Mully took off running and landed on third base with both feet. "Third base," she called, jumping up and down once again just for the joy of jumping around.

AJ came over and tapped the base with his foot.

"We really doing this?" he asked.

"Oh yeah," Mully said.

Without having to say another word they both sprinted for home plate. AJ had to hold his pants up a little to keep from tripping, but his legs were longer than Mully's and they ran neck and neck. As they got closer, they started pushing each other, trying to gain advantage, and they crossed the plate together in a tangle.

"Fine, fine, truce," AJ said, pulling free.

"Sucker." Mully stuck out her tongue.

"Well, we did it," he said once he had recovered his breath.

"What?"

"We rounded the bases."

"Oh for—that is not what happened!" Mully argued. She had forgotten what had started this whole thing anyway. For a few moments there, time had melted away and they hadn't been any particular age or any particular type of relationship. It had just been the two of them. Adam and Joey. AJ and Mully. Something clicked in Mully's brain, and she finally knew what she wanted.

"First of all, genius, we started at second so we DIDN'T round the bases," she laid into him. "Besides..." she trailed off and turned away.

"What?" It was AJ's turn to ask, somewhat annoyed.

Her voice was soft and she had her filmmaker face on as she looked around. "This wouldn't be the best visual on this field," she said.

AJ watched her back as she shifted her weight between her feet. "What visual are you talking about?" he asked.

Mully started wandering across the infield, slowly spinning around to take in every angle.

At last, she started speaking. "Well, that kiss is so iconic because they're sitting on the rock, right? But here, come on, come over here and look back at home plate. It's ugly! A chain link fence and half a high school? It's a bad visual, I'm telling you."

AJ came over and stood next to her.

"Ok hotshot, then where should our first kiss be?" He looked down at her and everything inside her grew hot at his words, hypothetical or not.

Mully considered the field. "Not at home plate." She shook her head. "And no big rocks available. But otherwise..." She spun around again. "Here?" she asked. She raised her hands, forming a rectangle just like they had seen directors do in behind-the-scenes documentaries and photos a million times. She smiled. "Here, if you look towards that side—"

"Right field," AJ mumbled.

"Whatever. Anyway, you've got the field but you've also got the woods, the rooftops... It's much better."

She grinned up at him.

"So..." He started to lean towards her but she stepped away, frowning again, and pulled up her rectangle hands.

Startled, AJ backed up a step as her hands swept past his face. She could have sworn disappointment flickered across his face, and he was breathing fast.

"But not very cinematic to just be standing in the field," she said, her heart racing.

She took his hand and led him onto the pitcher's mound. His shoulders were stiff, as if he had stopped breathing, and he looked down at their hands in disbelief. His hand was warm and big, encompassing her entire hand.

"IF you were going to film a first kiss in this field," she told him quietly, though her voice rang with confidence, "you would do it here, with the camera set up right there," she pointed. "Start slightly high and then lower it until it was below—"

She never finished her description of the shot. Their lips found each other's and as their eyes closed, neither of them saw the perfect background she had chosen.

31. Jamboree

"The River" had been the teen hang-out spot in Norford for over a hundred years, but every generation acted like they had invented gathering and drinking there. The Norford River itself wasn't terribly impressive, maybe thirty or forty feet across and slow moving. It skirted the right edge of the town all the way down until it spilled into Long Island Sound. Most of the crossing spots were boring bridges where the road simply continued over the river. But for some reason, some unknown hero had decided that the WPA would build one beautiful bridge over the Norford River. A brick arch spanned the crossing, and a wide, smooth cement top ran along both side railings. It also had four huge columns, two at each end, with elaborate eagles carved into stone shields watching over the banks. This art was almost completely unappreciated because it was on the crossing that saw the least traffic in the whole town: one side of the river had been declared too marshy to build houses on, and the other side was a wetland preserve. So this bridge, and the huge shadows that it cast, sat alone with the nearest house almost a mile away. And although the land might not have been safe to build on, it was plenty solid enough to support the weight of a car. Or rather, several cars.

Tonight, it was packed with cars parked in a more organized manner than usual. Instead of being scattered all over the grass of the riverbank, they were in two rows, forming a road between them that paralleled the actual, paved one. Jessica's minivan eased into a spot, and two other cars nearby began spilling out soon-to-be college freshmen as well. Trin hesitated in the van door for a moment, taking in the scene, until Megan piped up, "Hello? are we going or what?" Trin quickly jumped down, followed by Will, Megan, and Sarah.

There were ten future Willer students that year. Trin tried to control her breathing as she walked nervously with her classmates between the blinding headlights of the parked cars. The cheers of the older students seemed deafening to her.

Out of the general noise, she clearly heard someone yell, "Yeah, Trin!" and she all but strained her neck whipping her head around to see who had said it. Ellen was there. *Of course*, she thought, relief flooding through her body. Ellen was still wearing the same clothes from before, but now she had thrown on her own black Willer hoodie that matched the one all the freshmen were still wearing backwards. She sat on the hood of her car, nursing a beer, and thankfully giving Trin just as much attention as anyone else.

Trin smiled back at Ellen in gratitude. She barely had time to get nervous again before they were standing at the edge of the bridge, facing the cars. Trin was vaguely aware that Jessica and the guy next to her, the evident leaders, were saying something to them. It all sounded kind of like the grownups in Charlie Brown cartoons; the words just weren't penetrating her brain.

Adrenaline rushed through her. She looked around at the other initiates and started blindly copying what they were doing, until she realized that what they were doing was taking off their shoes and climbing up onto the wide stone railing of the bridge.

The kids farthest along inched towards the middle of

the river so that there was plenty of room for everyone on the ledge.

"What is going on?" Trin said, to the whole world rather than any one particular person.

"We just have to jump into the river," Megan said from a few feet away. "No biggie."

"*No biggie?*" Trin squeaked.

She was standing on the road of the bridge, well, hopping on one foot because she hadn't quite gotten her second shoe off, and she was seriously considering putting her other sneaker back on and going home. What would they do to her? Nothing. She could just put her leg down and walk calmly out of here... Trin glanced back at Ellen. She yanked her laces loose and took off her shoe. She had to wiggle awkwardly in her oversized, backwards sweatshirt, but she managed to get her messenger bag off too, and she dropped everything onto the growing pile of shoes in the middle of the bridge.

She looked at the tall railing uncertainly.

Will was already up on the railing. "Here," he said, offering her a hand.

"Thank you," she said shakily before scrambling up with a grunt. She stuck her hands out to her sides to steady herself. Trin looked down at the water. It looked like a solid black mass. There was no way it looked deep enough to jump into. When illuminated only by flashlights and car headlights, the river was downright menacing.

All those years I wanted to be cool enough to hang out at the river, Trin thought, *and now I'm here and probably going to die.*

Nikki was running point for Jessica and the boys' leader. "Quiet, please! Everyone... Hey, shut up!" she hollered.

"Ashley, turn that down." The music that had been filling the air disappeared.

"Thank you," Nikki yelled before turning to Jessica. "They're all yours."

Jessica cleared her throat so she could speak loudly enough, her voice echoing across the water now that everyone was silent. "Ladies and gentlemen, the class of 2004!"

Cheers erupted once again from the people gathered on the shore.

"You all know why you're here, so let's just do this, shall we?" Jessica continued. "Willer College was founded in 1853, blah blah blah, the first graduating class was 57% Norford High graduates, blah blah, go out and change the world, etcetera etcetera. Ok! Scott," she said, turning to the guy next to her, "Count 'em down!"

"Three!" Scott bellowed.

"Oh man," Will whispered nervously, looking down at the river gently flowing along about twelve feet below them.

"Two!"

Will looked wildly at Trin. "Are we crazy to do this?"

"One!" Scott yelled.

Like the other nine kids on the railing, Trin bent her knees. Just as she did, she realized that she was actually going to jump. Up until that moment, it had been a toss-up but she didn't even need to make a conscious decision: her knees did it for her. Trin closed her eyes and whispered out loud, "There is no museum in Iskenderun."

"What?" she heard Will ask.

"Jump!" Scott commanded.

They leapt.

There was a moment of freefall, when Trin's mind went blissfully blank, and then she splashed into the river. For a moment, the cold water swallowed her up completely. It was totally black. But it only took two kicks of her legs to bring her head up to the surface. She bobbed there, the black Willer hoodie ballooning around her.

Will surfaced nearby. Trin caught his eye and they started laughing at the sheer joy of what they'd just done. All around them, the heads of their classmates bobbed as they started trying to doggie paddle back to the shore.

"Your makeup!" Sarah gasped at Megan, who had mascara running down her cheeks.

"YOUR makeup!" Megan yelled back, splashing her. It turned into a massive water fight.

Up on the bridge, Jessica clinked beer cans with Scott in a toast. "Another successful year," she said, watching the chaos in the water below.

32. Sour Girl

Mully had to stop kissing AJ to gasp for air. He simply moved his lips down to her neck in the meantime. It was a few moments before she trusted herself to speak.

"AJ?"

"Mm-hmm?"

She looked up at the stars then closed her eyes. "I want to sleep with you."

He stopped, waited for her to open her eyes and smile, and kissed her harder than ever.

"I'm serious," Mully managed to break free to say. It had taken all her courage to say that out loud: knowing it could ruin everything with her best friend and deciding that it was still worth the risk. In these past minutes, as they kissed, it was as if everyone else in the world had disappeared... and when it was just her and AJ, it seemed so patently obvious that they should be together. It wasn't even a question of right or wrong. It just was. The two of them with their arms wrapped around each other made sense in a way that blocked out all other considerations, and Mully knew this night was *the* night. Or, well, the incredibly early morning.

"Thank god," AJ said.

He started to pull her down to the ground.

"Not here!" she gasped.

"Why not?"

"Anyone who comes around this side of the school will

see us," she pointed out.

"No they won't." He was trying to tug her down with one hand and undo his belt with the other. Neither operation was going well.

Mully ripped her arm free and put her hands on her hips, fighting back her laughter at how ridiculous he looked. "Oh my god, you're dumb," she said down to AJ now kneeling in front of her. "Yes, they would. We're on top of a small hill in the middle of a dark field."

"Yeah... dark."

"But *we* are not. We're the palest people ever. We probably glow in the dark." Mully also wondered how much longer it would be dark for. It had to be 4am already, and she had no idea when the sky would start lightening up for dawn.

"So leave your clothes on," AJ said, reaching a hand up along the back of her leg.

She laughed, partly because he was tickling her and partly at his suggestion. "I know I'm the virgin, but I'm sure leaving our clothes ON wouldn't work."

"Fine." AJ stood up and tried to wipe some of the reddish dirt off his jeans. He ignored her mention of the fact that he had had sex before and she hadn't. "Do you want to go back to the car?" he asked.

"No, I want to stay outside. Besides, there are people over there..."

"You ashamed of me?"

"Of course I am," Mully teased. "You think I want anyone knowing I slept with a loser like you?"

AJ wrapped his arms around her. "I love you," he whispered.

"I know," she whispered back.

They were just about to start kissing again when the

moment was ruined by the woods behind the field exploding with rustling noises.

"What the hell was that?" AJ shrieked, instinctively lowering himself into a crouch.

"Oh, cool!" Mully said, still standing. "It's a—oh for God's sake, will you calm down?" she added when she noticed him cowering behind her. "It's just a deer."

AJ stood and grabbed his shirt over his heart dramatically. "I think I just had a heart attack."

Mully started walking down from the mound in the direction of the deer as slowly as she could to keep from scaring it.

"I've never been this close to one before," she whispered back to AJ.

"There's two," he said, following her. "Probably a mom and her kid."

"A doe and her fawn," Mully corrected him.

"I knew that. I just wasn't showing off."

"Sure you did."

They stopped just a bit past the infield dirt, not wanting to scare the deer off. It was a doe and fawn, happily munching along the edge of the woods, working their way away from the high school past all the various playing fields.

Mully folded her arms across her chest to keep a little warmer. AJ came up behind her and put his arms around her. He was wearing her work shirt. She was wearing his flannel shirt. They watched the deer until they disappeared in the darkness.

"AJ?" Mully tipped her head back against him, feeling the warmth of his body (a new feeling and yet one she instantly fell in love with). Mully worried she might melt with happiness before they got to have sex. "I have an idea," she pressed on.

"What?" he asked without moving.

"Isn't there a soccer field down there?" She was looking at where the deer had disappeared.

"How would I know?"

"We went to this school for four years. How can we not know these things?"

"I mean, there was a soccer team. There's got to be a field somewhere but I—"

Mully broke free and started walking away from him.

"Where are you going?" he said, jogging to catch up with her.

"To find out," she said, grabbing his hand.

Both of them tried to pretend it didn't feel weird to be holding hands as they walked back across the outfield. Mully led them straight toward the woods, but before they reached the trees, they halted at the top of a steep hill, looking down at a grassy practice field with soccer goals at each end. It wasn't nearly as well-kept as the fields closer to the school, and the only light was a swarm of fireflies in the trees that surrounded the other three sides from the hill.

She grinned at him. "Told you."

"So why would you want me to see this soccer field?" AJ said, still a little annoyed. He looked down and recognition began to dawn on his face. "This... lovely, private, out of sight of the school, surrounded by woods soccer field," he finished, grinning back at her.

Without another word, they both started running down the hill, ignoring the staircase built into the incline. It was so steep that they had to let go of each other's hands to keep their balance as they launched themselves down to the field.

Mully was laughing like a kid as she reached the bottom. She stepped out of her boots and took off the flannel shirt. AJ had taken off his shirt as he ran and now spread it on the grass.

"M'lady," he said, bowing low and gesturing her to the shirt.

Mully sat down, trying to line up as much of her body with the shirt as possible. AJ scrambled to pull his undershirt over his head while she wasn't looking at him. They both tried not to laugh as they lay down and resumed making out. It lasted both forever and was over in a moment as things escalated until they were both naked.

Mully tried not to marvel at the fact that she had never seen AJ naked before. They had spent so much time together. Slept in each other's beds. She had hung out in the bathroom while he was peeing plenty of times, but even then she had only seen a little of him. Now here he was, on top of her, pressing her down so that she felt the cold of the grass beneath them through the thin cotton shirt.

He too seemed to realize they had reached the point of no return, because he stopped kissing her and propped himself up on his elbows. He gently bumped his nose against hers so that they were staring right into each other's eyes when he asked, "You're sure?"

"Of course I'm sure. Who else would it be?" Mully had to resist the urge to roll her eyes or laugh or anything that might break the spell of AJ nuzzling his nose against her face, against her neck, kissing her again.

"I've waited so long for this," he breathed onto her skin.

Mully didn't answer. She stared up at the fading stars and let the feeling wash over her.

33. Train Song

Trin clambered out of the river and Nikki came over to wrap a towel around her shoulders. Various kids were doing the same for the rest of the drenched initiates. Trin went over to sit against someone's car's bumper and shivered, grateful for the towel. She marveled that the night that had seemed so pitch black before she jumped was now light enough that no one needed flashlights to see anymore. The sky was lightening and she smiled at the new day. Even the music was mellower now as Phish drifted across the scattered cars that were left at The River. Nikki came back over and handed Trin an already-opened beer.

"Your reward," she said with a wink.

"Thanks," Trin said, taking it.

She clinked the bottle against Nikki's but didn't drink any.

"Trin! I'm so proud of you!" Ellen came running up to her.

"You mean Kat?" Nikki said.

"Are you going by Kat now?" Ellen asked her.

Trin shrugged and then had to grab at the towel as it slipped. "I might."

"I love it," Ellen said. "Kat. Cool choice."

Nikki wandered off when someone called her name from a few cars down. Ellen sat next to Trin on the car's bumper.

"You sticking around, or do you want to get home and dry off?" Ellen asked.

Trin looked down at the beer in her hand. "I don't drink so... I should probably go home. But I have to go get my car."

"Where are you parked?"

"The diner."

"No problem," Ellen said, pushing up off the bumper.

"Can I get a ride?" Will asked. Trin hadn't even noticed him standing nearby.

"Don't you want to stay?" she asked him.

"It's dawn, which means I've been awake for twenty-four hours. I am *done*. I just want to get dry, climb into bed, and fall asleep for the next week."

"You can come with us," Trin said without thinking, then added, "I mean, if Ellen doesn't mind."

"One wet kid in my car, two wet kids, what's the difference?" Ellen laughed. "Where do you live?" she asked Will.

"Bartleby. Right by the diner, so I won't even be taking you out of your way really."

"Hop in," Ellen waved them toward her Porsche.

Trin balanced her untouched beer on the bumper of the car, a present to some unknown stranger, and followed Will and Ellen. Like Will, she was carrying her shoes and walking around barefoot. She waited for Will to climb into the backseat before sitting in the passenger seat, careful not to get her towel caught in the door.

"You ok back there?" she asked Will.

"Never better," he said, grinning.

"Next time I come to one of these things," Ellen muttered, "I'll remember to bring extra blankets and towels."

She sighed, glancing down at the upholstery on Trin's seat, then she started the car. The radio blasted them with "My Name Is" before Ellen could scramble at the volume knob to turn it down. "Sorry," she said.

Trin laughed and settled more comfortably into her seat as they drove away from the river and got out onto the road.

34. I Want You to Want Me

After a minute, Ellen asked, "So, how's it feel to be part of the Willer College student body?"

"It feels good." Trin smiled. She felt comfortable about going to college in a way that she hadn't last night.

"It's excellent," Will added.

Ellen glanced at him in her rearview mirror. "Do you know what you're going to college for yet?"

"Not a clue!" he laughed. "Something with numbers but not, like, straight up math."

"What about you?" she asked Trin.

Trin sat silently for a moment, thinking, but when she spoke her voice was clear. "English. I'm going to be a writer."

"Not a famous movie director?" Ellen teased.

"No. I'll, uh, leave that to Mully."

Trin snuggled happily into her towel, cozy now that she was a little drier and the car was warming up.

"Write screenplays," Ellen commanded her. "Mully's ass owes you for the past four years so she'll have to buy them, right?"

"Maybe," Trin said.

All too soon, Ellen was pulling into the diner parking lot. She stopped right next to Trin's car and put the car in park. They both turned and looked at Will in the backseat, who was asleep.

Ellen pointed and mouthed, "*You? Him? A thing?*"

Trin blushed and shook her head no.

"Do you want to be the one who takes him home?" Ellen whispered.

"That's ok," Trin replied. "That'd be kind of weird to switch this close to his house."

"So what? He was looking at you. He totally wouldn't mind."

"Really, it's fine." Trin wasn't sure how she knew this, but she was feeling much more certain of things this morning. "We can, like, get to know each other at school."

"Ok then," Ellen whispered. She winked at Trin, took a deep breath and bellowed, "Ok Will! You're up next! What's your address?"

Will jerked awake, arms and legs flailing in shock.

"Wha—where am I?" he asked, blinking in the ever-brightening dawn light.

Ellen turned around toward him. "We're at the diner but Trin's about to get out and I need to know your address to take you home."

"I'm not going with you?" Will asked Trin, still looking confused.

"Uh, no, Will. Ellen will drop you off in like two minutes."

"Oh, ok, sure," he said, rubbing his eyes. "Well, I'll see you on campus. On campus!" He sat up, rejuvenated with excitement. "I love it. See you around campus, Kat. Trin. You."

Trin got out of the car and didn't realize Will was already climbing forward into the passenger seat. When she leaned back into the car to say goodbye, she only just managed to avoiding colliding into him face-first.

Which meant that her face was inches from Will's as

she said, "See you Will." Startled, she jerked backward and barely remembered to say, "Bye Ellen."

Ellen leaned forward so that Trin would see the grin on her face as she told her, "You are too good at this."

"Huh?" Will looked back and forth between them, still not fully awake.

"Nothing!" Trin squeaked. "Good *night* Ellen," she hissed as she closed the door on them.

"It's morning!" Will shouted with a laugh out the open window.

She waved as they drove away. Trin looked carefully around for any minivans before unlocking her car door. It was just starting to catch up with her how tired she really was. Trin tossed her Chucks into the backseat and stripped off her wet Willer sweatshirt and threw it back there too. She used the towel to dry her arms before carefully folding it and placing it on her seat. At last, she climbed in and settled into her car.

She wiggled her toes before stepping down on the brake barefoot and starting the car. She had left the *10 Things I Hate About You* soundtrack in the CD player and she hit the back button to restart the first song. Trin smiled at herself in the rearview mirror. She looked like an utter mess but she couldn't help grinning. She put the car into reverse and drove off into the dawn.

35. This is Just a Modern Rock Song

Mully and AJ were also driving around in the brightening morning. It was seven now and the sun was fully shining down on Norford, though the streets were still quiet. Neither of them said anything, but both were trying not to get caught smiling by the other as they sped down an empty Post Road.

AJ was the first to crack and speak. "You're sure you want to leave now?" he asked her.

"AJ..." she said warningly.

"Just saying."

"I've only got... five hours until my flight."

AJ scoffed. "Five hours, that's plenty of time to— you're blushing!"

It took all of Mully's concentration to keep driving and deny it.

"I am not."

"You totally are," AJ said, half laughing.

He looked like he wanted to say more, but they were already on his street and before she knew it, she was pulling into his driveway. AJ undid his seatbelt and reached into the backseat. Mully's old shirt lay back there in a crumpled pile; it was muddy and wet and he hadn't wanted to put it back on afterwards. AJ gathered up his CD binder, the tape recorder, and the extra flannel shirt, grunting with the effort it took to lift his CDs from the backseat one-handed. Mully tried not to look at the bit of his stomach that was revealed by his contortions, but she did. And she liked it. She smiled to herself, realizing she was totally objectifying her best friend. Last night had changed the way she looked at him, the way she watched him move, but she knew AJ still her friend. That remained the same.

She quickly rearranged her face and stared straight ahead out her windshield as he sat back down with his stuff in his lap.

"Well, this is it," he said when she just kept looking at his garage's door.

"Oh, this is yours," she said, starting to take off her flannel.

"Keep it."

"You sure?" Mully asked.

"You wear it more often than I do anyway. My gift to you," he said.

"Well, thanks," she said, shrugging it back over her shoulders.

"So..." He made no move to get out of the car.

"So..." she echoed him.

They stared at each other before both awkwardly leaning in at the same moment. Their lips met over the center console. It wasn't bad, but it wasn't passionate either. Just a simple kiss before AJ drew away and cleared his throat, gathering up his things in his arms.

He had his hand on the door handle before he turned back to her and said, "Be good."

"Always," Mully told him. She bit her lip as soon as AJ's back was turned. There was a little voice inside her that wished it were more, that wanted to shout out, "I love you" or "Come with me to California", but the logical part of her brain was winning out. She *did* love him, but she also knew he was going to go into his house now and she was going to let him without saying anything else.

AJ got out of her car and all but skipped up to his front door. The change in him from last night when she picked him up was unmistakable. AJ was *happy*, and Mully let herself accept the warm blush she felt growing inside her as she thought about how he was happy because of *her*. He fumbled his keys out of his pocket to unlock the front door and let himself in.

AJ turned in the doorway and waved. Mully waved through the windshield, trying to shove down the aching feeling that she had just passed up a once-in-a-life opportunity. Then he went inside and closed the door behind him, and the screen door slammed shut a second later. Mully sat there, just thinking. Or trying to think. She frowned. There was no way she could gather her thoughts while stationary.

She grabbed a CD at random and put it in before pulling out of AJ's driveway. She drove down his street, trying to convince herself that she was in the mood for Bif Naked, before finally shaking her head in frustration. She didn't know what to think or feel or do at this moment, and this wasn't helping. She didn't understand how she could be so sure that it was right to drive away and stay friends when she had to fight her arms from pulling the car around and going back and trying for a kiss with more heat between them.

Mully stopped at the end of AJ's street and took a moment to change the CD. This one was *not* doing it. She popped in the mix Ana had given her. She didn't recognize the first song even after she had looked at the track listing. The band name was sort of familiar, but she'd never heard this before. Early '90s alt rock led by a sweet woman's voice filled her car, and Mully felt herself relax. Yes, this pop-ish nonsense was just what she needed.

She turned right and suddenly stopped again. On the cross street, where it was legal to street park, was Ana's car. An awful icy feeling flowed from Mully's head down through her whole body. The last thing she did before going completely numb was to look over her shoulder down AJ's street toward his house.

36. Spin the Bottle

Ana had driven herself home after leaving the diner, pulling her car into the driveway and setting off the motion-sensor for the floodlight. After she let herself into the house, she tiptoed upstairs. Through her parents' bedroom door, Ana heard her father turn over in bed. Their window looked out over the driveway, so he could always tell by the floodlight when she got home, but apparently he had decided that her breaking curfew wasn't worth getting out of bed tonight. With a smile, she continued on to her room.

Bilbo was sleeping on her desk chair and barely stirred as she changed into a too-big t-shirt and boxer shorts for bed. She crept back out down the hallway to the bathroom, not turning on the light until after she had closed the door behind her. She took two steps, then sighed as she felt litter under her feet. With a grimace, she cleaned the cat's litter box before using the bathroom herself and brushing her teeth. Ana brushed harder than she'd meant to because halfway through, she remembered that her toothbrush had Princess Leia on it and AJ had bought it for her. It made her slightly furious, and she took it out on her gums. She reassured herself that in her room, she had already packed a new toothbrush for college that had absolutely nothing to do with her ex-boyfriend.

Back in her room, Ana climbed into bed and tried to sleep. She tossed and turned and ended up staring at the neat pile of boxes, milk crates, and tote bags stuffed to bursting which she had packed up for tomorrow's move. Hot tears flooded her eyes and she let herself cry again, because she finally realized *why* she was so mad. She was mad at AJ for not telling her the truth, but she was much, much madder at herself for being so stupid. Now it was so obvious that AJ had never been planning to go to college with her. Where had his letter from his future roommate been? Why didn't he need to go find Twin XL sheets? He hadn't been packing at all this summer!

Ana lay in her bed feeling hopelessly stupid for not putting it together on her own. She thought of the framed photos of her and AJ, carefully packed among her sweaters in one of those boxes. A large one from last year's winter formal, a small candid Mully had taken that was her favorite photo of the two of them, and another of Ana hugging AJ in the music hallway after a show, with her still in crazy stage makeup and AJ all in black with his headset around his neck.

As the tears subsided, Ana stared at her bedroom ceiling and wondered if she should go unpack those pictures. Then, with a thought that made her whole chest ache, she realized that she didn't want to. She loved those photos and she loved AJ and she loved the two of them together. The difficulty of holding that truth right alongside the truth that she was incredibly mad at him for lying to her out of cowardice felt like it would split her body apart.

But it didn't.

She sighed and rolled over to turn on her bedside lamp. There was no way she could sleep. She picked up the book she'd been reading and put it back down without even attempting to open it. It was AJ's ability with words, the magic of watching him create a whole world out of nothing, which had been what really made her fall for him. Ana pushed herself up out of bed and pulled on her sweatshirt. She grabbed her mini-backpack that had her wallet and keys in it and slipped on her shoes. She realized she hadn't unpacked her bag, as if part of her brain knew she'd be going back out. She quickly flipped open a notebook on her desk and scribbled, "At AJ's. I promise I'll be back in time" on the first page. She left that on her bed so her parents wouldn't panic.

Then she crept back outside, drove herself almost to AJ's, and parked the car around the corner from his house. The house was built into a hill so all she had to do was walk around into the backyard and she was right at AJ's bedroom window. Last summer, he had started leaving the screen slightly ajar in one corner so that she could wiggle a finger in and open it from the outside. Ana tried not to wonder if any of his neighbors had noticed her essentially breaking into the Cadwallyns' house over and over again. Instead, she pulled herself up and into his room.

AJ wasn't there. But he had said he was going to stay up until sunrise with Mully, so she wasn't surprised. Ana didn't know when exactly dawn was, but the sky was still dark, only just barely beginning to lighten, so she probably had another half hour or so. She walked over to his bookcase and grabbed one of AJ's Star Wars expanded universe novels at random. She turned on his bedside lamp and lay down to read until he got back, letting a smile spread across her face as she imagined his look when he came in and saw her on his bed again.

AJ tiptoed up the stairs and stumbled through his living room. Their dog lifted his head and the tags on his collar jangled.

"Shhhh, good boy," AJ said, scratching behind his ear. Chewie sighed deeply and lay back down. AJ glanced gratefully down the hallway at his parents' closed bedroom door. He just had to make it past Jack's room. Jack was probably asleep, but there was always the chance that he was up and looking to bust his little brother. AJ let his dog drift back to sleep, eased his way past Jack's bedroom door, and breathed a sigh of relief. He opened his door and stopped short.

Ana was sitting on his bed.

"Hi," she said softly.

AJ rushed into his room and closed the door silently behind him. He took a step toward her, then hesitated. The morning light poured through his open bedroom window behind her, making a sort of halo all around her skin and hair. He had known she was gorgeous. Now she looked like an angel.

Ana smiled at him encouragingly.

He was very aware of his terrible breath and the fact that he was still wearing his clothes from yesterday. He was also very aware that he needed a shower after having sex with Mully.

AJ took a few steps closer. He should say something, he

should explain. She was still smiling and AJ wondered if she was she here to get back together with him? Did he want to? He certainly couldn't get back together with Ana without telling her about last night... could he?

She reached her hand out and pulled him the last few feet so that he was standing right in front of her.

"I have a few hours before I leave," Ana said, that little teasing tone in her voice that always drove him wild.

Tell her, his brain screamed. *Tell her you're with Mully.* But he didn't open his mouth. After all, he told himself, w*as* he with Mully? It had been one night on a soccer field. Okay, a great night, but Mully hadn't said much afterwards and now she was on her way to California and he was here. And so was Ana.

He reached out and tucked a loose strand of her hair back behind an ear. She didn't stop him and AJ felt his heart start racing as he realized he was getting a second chance. Before he could even process how stupidly lucky he was, Ana reached up and pulled his mouth down to hers. They fell onto the bed in a familiar tangle, trying to be quiet.

38. I Turn to You

At the end of AJ's street, Mully's car was stopped in the middle of the road as she stared in shock at Ana's BMW parked on the side of the street. She knew she couldn't just sit here, but she wasn't sure she was capable of moving. Ana was at AJ's. AJ was at AJ's. Which meant...

What does it mean? she wondered to herself. Really. What had last night meant in the grand scheme of things?

She couldn't think straight. It was all too soon, too real. She licked her lips, then realized she tasted like AJ.

In frustration, Mully slammed her open palms against her steering wheel. *She* had just driven AJ home, and *she* was the one who let him get out of the car, so *she* did not get to feel a little whiff of betrayal as she imagined him kissing Ana, Mully told herself. She couldn't help it though.

A car drove up behind and honked at her. Mully jerked out of her trance and waved an apology before she put the car in drive, but she pulled over as soon as possible to let the guy go by. She drove slowly, unsure what to do. Mully realized she was still listening to the CD Ana had made her and started laughing. It was just so absurd. They had all been tangled up together and now...

Mully slowed to a stop and let her body shake with her laughter. She laughed at how ridiculous she felt being jealous of Ana. She laughed at how good it had felt to finally kiss AJ. A few tears squeezed out as she laughed. Because she was also laughing at how crazy last night had been: a million things had to happen just right for her to end up with AJ on that soccer field—and they had! It was like the universe wanted it to happen. But apparently the universe didn't want things to stay that way, because now she was back in her car alone, AJ and Ana were probably getting back together, and she felt in her bones that it was time to go get on a plane and experience something else new.

Mully glanced at herself in the rearview mirror. She was a disaster. She tried to run her hand through her hair to neaten it, but it was hopeless. She quickly pulled a hair elastic off her wrist and threw her hair up into a ponytail instead.

That completed, she sat up a little straighter and headed home.

Mully slowed down as she approached her house and stared at Ellen's car parked in Mully's usual spot on the driveway. Even more shocking, Ellen was coming out of the garage, waving and shouting something at her. Mully turned down "Freak on a Leash" enough to hear what Ellen was saying as she pulled into the driveway.

"Turn around dum dum. Dad says to back into the garage before you leave." Ellen lit a cigarette and leaned against her Porsche while Mully complied.

The surprises weren't over. Mully backed her Jag into the garage and looked over to see that her sister had been working on the Dino. In a daze, she turned off her engine— then realized this was the last time she would be in her own car for a while. She gathered up her CD player, the CD holder from her visor, her sunglasses from the glove compartment, and her old work shirt from the backseat. Until her sister told her to pull the car in the garage, Mully hadn't really processed that this was it: she wouldn't be driving her car again for months. She worried about her parents thinking it messy, but of course she kept the interior immaculate, even after being out all night with her friends.

Ellen threw away her cigarette butt and edged around the Jag back to what she had been working on. She had brought her boombox into the garage and was playing Christina Aguilera. When Mully made a face as she got out of her car, Ellen snapped, "Last time Dad picked the music. This time, I pick the music, ok?"

"I guess I won't be here to care one way or another," Mully said sadly, clutching her stuff to her chest.

Ellen had been about to turn away, but instead asked, "You ok?"

"I'm fine," Mully said too quickly.

"Ok, spill," Ellen commanded, folding her arms across her chest and leaning against her car. "What happened? Did AJ declare his love for you or something?"

Mully winced. Ellen's expression melted and she opened her mouth to say something, but Mully started speaking instead.

"Did you... When you and Jack were... Was he..." Mully gave up on getting a question out and dumped her stuff on her car hood instead, letting her frustration travel up her spine and out through her arms.

"Jack was technically my first, but I'd already done a lot," Ellen told her, thankfully putting a quick end to her torture.

Mully nodded.

Ellen let out a low whistle. "Wow. Ok. So AJ huh?"

"He and Ana broke up at the carnival." Ellen's eyes widened but she didn't say anything as Mully continued, "But we hung out and then Ana was at the diner anyway so all four of us were just, you know, normal, but then the others had to go home so AJ and I hung out. Just the two of us."

"And..." Ellen said softly.

Mully just nodded.

"Wow," Ellen repeated herself.

"But now I don't know... because I think he and Ana are going to get back together and—" Mully's eyes stung and began to fill with tears. Ellen launched herself up and grabbed Mully in a tight hug.

"Hey sis? Can I make a suggestion?"

"Yeah," Mully muttered into Ellen's arm.

"Fuck 'em."

Mully pulled back and Ellen let go of her.

"I'm serious," Ellen said, pulling a pencil out from behind her ear with one hand and picking up a clipboard with her other, ready to get back to work. "How many times did Jack and I break up and get back together again? For all I know, we'll still get back together someday, and I'll spend the freaking rest of my life in Norford. I mean, Mully, I have to ask: was it good?"

Mully, still stunned, shrugged then nodded.

"So, great! Awesome. Now go inside and eat some breakfast and finish packing and get on a plane to California and move on with your life."

"But—"

"No buts. That's the advice. I don't mean to toot my own horn, but it's good advice too."

And Ellen turned around as if that were all there was to say about it.

Curiosity won out. "What are you doing?" Mully asked.

"Dad wants a list of everything that needs to be done," Ellen said without looking up from her clipboard.

"Do you really think it's possible to fix it?"

Ellen sighed. "It might not be." She looked sadly at the engine damage where a tree had dissected the front of her car. "But it might. And wouldn't it be cool to have it back up and running for its 30th anniversary?"

"Sure would," Mully said. She picked her stuff back up. It hadn't exactly been the sisterly heart-to-heart she had hoped for when Ellen followed her into the garage, but she did feel a little better.

39. Everything You Want

For someone whose family drove the most iconic cars in Norford, Mr. Carr had been driving the most boring beige sedan for most of Ellen and Mully's lives. He had pulled up in the unloading zone of LaGuardia Airport and taken her suitcase and bags out of the trunk while Mully hugged her mother good-bye.

She turned to her dad.

"You're sure you don't want me to wait with you?" he offered for the thousandth time.

"Dad!" Mully rolled her eyes in embarrassment. "I'll be fine. And you guys don't want to waste your day hanging out here."

"We would have, happily," he swore, pulling her into a tight hug.

Mully felt like she could start crying any moment.

"Go be amazing," her dad whispered, squeezing her even harder.

"Love you, dad," she whispered back.

She managed not to cry, barely, and pulled free of his embrace.

Mully had saved her sarcastic awesome sister for last; she turned to Ellen, who was leaning against the car.

"Stay safe," Ellen said, throwing an arm around her and squeezing her close for a moment.

"Be amazing," Mully smiled. It was what their parents

had always said to both of them. "Keep an eye on these two troublemakers for me."

"Will do," Ellen said, letting go of her.

Mully pulled her backpack up onto a shoulder and picked up her duffel and suitcase. She stood looking at her family.

"Ok, uh, see ya Ellen. Bye... guys."

"Call us the minute you land," her mom said.

"I will." Mully nodded her head for emphasis. If her hands had been free, she would have saluted. "Well... yeah. Bye."

She turned and walked toward the terminal entrance. Mully peeked over her shoulder back at the car. Her dad was walking around back to the driver's seat, but her mom and Ellen saw her looking and waved. She nodded in acknowledgment and walked into the airport.

Inside, Mully crossed her fingers for luck as her bags were weighed to make sure they were under the weight limit— she made it, with a whole pound and a half to spare. She took her boarding pass and walked over to security.

The guard running the metal detector waved her over to the right line and she dropped her backpack onto the conveyor belt before walking through.

And here she was: off on her adventure, ready to begin the rest of her life!

Mully looked at the big clock on the wall: she had over an hour before her flight. With a groan, she grabbed her backpack and started wandering around. A few minutes ago, she had been almost crying saying goodbye to her dad, but now she was annoyed that he always insisted on getting to the airport so early. Mully grimaced at the pop music playing over the loudspeaker with frequent squeaky, indecipherable interruptions.

She ended up sitting at her gate, eating candy, and listening to Nerf Herder on her Discman. It was a decent spot for people-watching. An idea struck her, and she went fishing in her backpack for a notebook and pen.

The notebook fell open to where a CD was tucked between the pages. Mully knew it was from AJ immediately. No one else would give someone a CD without even a case or envelope to protect it. Plus, it was his handwriting that said "Do Not Open Until Airborne" in Sharpie on the disc. For a second, Mully couldn't figure out how it got there, but then she remembered AJ being in her room last night. Before they went to the diner. Before...

Mully tapped the CD against her leg a few times, debating playing it now. She frowned at the CD, then, laughing at herself, she shoved it into her CD holder. It was the same one she had kept on her car's sun visor, and it was just short enough to fit standing up in her backpack. It was already full, but she was able to slip the disc in with another CD. Then she forced herself to turn her mind back to the notebook and uncap her pen to start writing.

40. Different People

Mully kept a death grip on her seat's arm rests through the takeoff, as if she personally were responsible for holding onto the airplane to keep things together. As she felt it level off, she relaxed and shot a smile in apology to the person sitting next to her in the aisle seat. They were still climbing, but more gently now, and no one tried to stop her when she reached down into her backpack under the seat in front of her and pulled out her Discman.

She chewed her Juicy Fruit as she put in the CD AJ had made her. Mully looked out her window and realized they were pointed north, right in the direction of Norford. Just as she was trying to think if that was symbolic or anything, the plane banked and turned westward. They were flying over New York City. Mully looked over the familiar skyline, a sight she had been in love with for as long as she could remember. NYC had always seemed like the most exciting, the most glamorous, simply the ultimate place on earth. Now they were passing the tip of Manhattan. She felt like she could reach out and touch the Statue of Liberty and World Trade Center. Mully didn't have any tears left in her after this morning's talk with Ellen, but she did let out a little sigh as she said goodbye to the East Coast. Finally, she sat back in her seat and pressed play on her CD player.

Instead of music, she heard AJ's voice. "Hiya Mully." She drew in a sharp breath at the sound of his voice, a million emotions rushing through her at once. "Well, I finally got a CD burner, so you can expect lots of excellent mixes in your mail this semester. And, no, I won't be labeling any of them, so get over it. I'm coming to you not-live from my room, August 1st in the year 2000. Before this month is over, you're going to leave, and it just—it feels like a piece of me is leaving. That sounds weird. I mean, we've never been apart like that before. I mean, I sort of—" he sighed, then continued, "I guess, the only way I can think to put it, is that I love you? But you already knew that. I mean, even if we don't say it like that—I mean obviously you're the most important person in the world to me, so... So anyway, you probably want the music, huh?

"Sorry I couldn't fit more than an hour on this CD, but it will tide you over until the movie starts. I hope. I can't believe you're going to USC. Just don't forget us, ok? You're going to see the world and change, and this place never changes. I know you need to do that. But just come back for Christmas. See you then. Have a good flight. Have a good life. Just kidding. Oh, and don't hate me for including No Doubt. I mean, California, right?"

The plane banked again and a ray of sunshine blinded Mully for a moment. When she could look back out the window, NYC wasn't in sight anymore. There were the usual two seconds of silence between tracks, then the ska music began blasting in Mully's ears. She had to stop herself from laughing out loud. For once, she didn't mind it at all.

Will Thomas looked up from his laptop and signaled the waitress for another cup of coffee. She was a pretty blonde and he debated flirting with her but settled for smiling. Then he forced himself to focus on what he was typing.

Somehow, he had been roped into helping with his ten-year high school reunion. The closer it got, the more emails he received. Now he was typing up the little bios everyone had submitted for the newsletter they would send out the month before. He guessed it was kind of cool to be the first person to see what everyone was up to. After Willer, Will had moved to Boston for grad school and lost touch with his friends other than seeing everyone's updates on social media. His parents had moved to North Carolina just a couple years after that, and he hadn't been back to Norford since.

Will was glad he had decided to pull off the highway and spend the afternoon visiting his hometown rather than speeding through to New York City like he usually did when going to visit his old college roommate in Brooklyn. One nice thing, he thought, looking around the diner, was that some things never changed. The mural portraying a drive-in was still painted on the side of the building, a cool retro red sports car was parked out front, and a group of teenagers were talking just a bit too loudly a couple booths over.

The waitress came back to his booth and he looked at her over his laptop screen. She seemed familiar so he figured they might have been in school together.

"What kind of pie do you like?" she asked.

"Uh..."

"On the house," she clarified.

He still felt awkward but he wasn't going to turn down free food. "Apple. Please."

She served it up and brought the plate over.

"You sure I won't get you in trouble?" he asked.

"I own the place," she laughed. "And I remember your initiation night at the river."

Will looked more closely at her face, but he had to cheat and glanced at her name tag.

"Ellen? So Ellen... Carr, right?"

"I was."

"Wowza!" Will laughed. "Oh my god, hi! How've you been?"

"Busy," Ellen shrugged.

"I'm so sorry, I didn't realize—"

She waved him off. "It happens. How are you doing?"

"I'm good. Moved. But you know, normal human being. Actually, Joey's your sister, right? I'm doing the bios for our reunion and I just got hers."

"Aww, how on earth did you get stuck doing that?" Ellen teased.

"Oh, I'm super lucky," Will deadpanned in return.

"Well, you're lucky enough for free pie. I gotta get back to work. Good to see you." Ellen went back behind the counter to tend to some of the regulars.

Will wolfed down over half the slice before getting back to his typing. He furrowed his brow in thought, and finally decided, yeah, no one was using titles in their names. He deleted the "Mrs." Ana Foster had submitted with her bio.

Guess someone insisted on keeping her name, he chuckled to himself as he wrote:

Ana Foster is an organization solution specialist with McKinsey & Company.

He hoped she wouldn't be too mad; Will had no doubts that Ana Foster could still be a little scary when she wanted to. Then he couldn't help glancing up at the entry above Ana's:

Katrina Foley (nee Edlund) is an English teacher at Newtown High School.

Will was looking forward to seeing lots of people at the reunion, but it was Kat was who he missed the most. They had stayed friends after Willer, but once she started grad school in Connecticut and he started working in Massachusetts, things had just gotten busy. They had drifted apart. She had still invited him to the wedding last year, but it happened to be the same weekend as his cousin's down in South Carolina, so the reunion would be his first chance to meet Kat's wife.

Will took another gulp of coffee before scrolling up to the C's to type in the latest entry he'd received:

Josephine Carr is an associate producer and mother of two.

Will smiled, remembering how flustered Kat would get that she still called Joey Carr "Mully" years after she had moved to California. Everyone who had gone to high school with her bragged about having known her before she got famous and worked with movie stars. Personally, Will was still more impressed by anyone his age that actually had *kids.* It was enough of a shock when someone posted pictures of their babies online, but Joey's twin sons were already in elementary school. Just thinking about attending college with babies at home made Will need a nap. He caught the eye of their "Aunt

Ellen" and motioned for more coffee.

Will hit save on his laptop and sat back in the booth to enjoy the rest of his pie. As he glanced outside, he saw a pack of teenagers piling out of two cars parked next to each other. They didn't dress like he and his friends had, and no one had bright blue hair, but Will smiled to see a group like that headed into the diner all the same.

"Thanks," he said to Ellen as she poured him a fresh cup. Will took a sip as he looked out the windows at the sun setting on the Post Road.

About the Author

Tierney Steele is a writer, podcaster, librarian, and sister. Her younger sibling refuses to refer to herself as SteeleSisterToo. Despite that disappointment, you can find Tierney at www.OneSteeleSister.com. Her podcasts are part of the "Movies by Minute" community. (Thanks Pete and Alex!) When she isn't deep-diving into films both classic and cult, Tierney can be found checking out the nearest museum or attending summer camp reunions. She lives near Boston with her husband, son, and a cat named after Cooperstown.

Lightning Source UK Ltd.
Milton Keynes UK
UKHW040721230522
403385UK00001B/54

9 798985 858181